THE SWAYING PILLARS

The merest chance presents Helena Sebright with a three-month job in the newly independent African state of Uyowa. She is to escort a seven-year-old girl on the journey to stay with her grandparents who live there, and to bring her back to her parents in England at the end.

It seems a lucky break. But then Helena is not to know that she will become involved in a dangerous criminal enterprise. Against the background of a disintegrating state, with guns in the streets and bloody revolution imminent, Helena finds herself caught up in a series of mysteries, catastrophes – and gruesome deaths . . .

THE SWAYING PILLARS

Elizabeth Ferrars

·BLACK·
DAGGER
·CRIME·

First published 1968
by
William Collins

This edition 2001 by Chivers Press
published by arrangement with
Peter MacTaggart

ISBN 0 7540 8593 7

Copyright © 1968 by Peter MacTaggart

British Library Cataloguing in Publication Data available

Printed and bound in Great Britain by
Bookcraft, Midsomer Norton, Somerset

TO GILDA AND JOHN

The country of Uyowa and its capital city of Tondolo and all the characters in this story are imaginary.

CHAPTER I

It was Cleo Grant who offered Helena Sebright the chance to go to Uyowa. The two of them met accidentally one evening in the Underground at Piccadilly. They were hurrying in different directions, saw one another at the same time, waved and each called out that she was in a terrible hurry now but that they must arrange to meet soon. Then they went on on their separate ways. But a moment later Helena felt her arm grabbed from behind and found Cleo beside her.

"Are you really in a hurry, Helena?" Cleo asked. "I've just thought of something I'd like to talk to you about."

Helena had only been going to a cinema to try to escape from a singularly bad mood, due to a row in the office, that had possessed her all day. Wherever Cleo had been going, she had decided to forget it. They went up into Shaftesbury Avenue together. The January evening was very cold. Raw gusts of wind came howling down the streets, digging sharp teeth into their ankles. The pavements were slimy from recent rain and there was a tang of possible snow in the air.

They went into Forte's, where it was reasonably warm, and ordered coffee. Cleo unbuttoned her coat and smoothed her hair back from her face. It was chestnut hair, fiery and sleek and long. Her coat was jade green and so was the dress that she was wearing under it and she had a big jade ring, set in silver, on one of her long, thin fingers. Her nail-varnish too was silver. She had always liked exotic colours and sharp contrasts. She was a tall, somewhat angular and not really beautiful girl, yet she had a way of making you think that she was beautiful by a certain bold grace of movement that she had and her brave show of self-confidence.

Helena, dressed now in a grey jersey dress, the sort of thing that they expected her to wear in her very conservative office, had often envied Cleo that apparent self-confidence, in spite of being one of the few people who knew that it was almost entirely false. Cleo was really a rather frightened person. She was frightened of all kinds of unexpected things, such as of being alone in a house at night, of learning to swim, of driving a car. And this was strange, for she had led anything but a sheltered life.

Until meeting Cleo, Helena had never realised how sheltered her own life had been. Her father was an Inspector of Schools, her mother was a psychiatric social worker. Helena had been sent to a progressive school, where she had had to decide for herself from an early age what she wanted to learn and what she did not; perhaps because of this had failed to get into a University, so had gone to a secretarial school; had had several serious love-affairs by the time she was twenty, from which she had emerged with the conviction that there was not much that life had to teach her. She had travelled a certain amount, hitch-hiking once to Barcelona and another time to Budapest, and for the last five years she had worked in a solicitor's office, where she had steadily been given more and more responsibility.

But Cleo had grown up in Kenya. Once, in the days of Mau Mau, she had only just escaped being murdered. She was the daughter of a wealthy coffee planter and had got engaged early to a Pole—or had he been a Hungarian? Anyway, he had been a refugee from his own country, a stateless man, who had had some unpronounceably Eastern European name and had simply disappeared when he heard that Cleo's rich father had gone bankrupt. But that had not been all that Cleo had had to endure. Her father had sent her away to friends, then had shot both her mother and himself with the revolver that had once saved them from the Mau Mau. Not long afterwards Cleo had come to London, had trained as a secretary in the same school as Helena and settled down to earning her living.

If settling down was what it could be called. She never stayed long in any job, any more than she could stick to any man for more than a month or two. She was attractive to men and was easily attracted by them and almost every time that Helena met her had just found someone with whom she knew that she would stay in love for ever. Yet by their next meeting Cleo would claim that she could hardly remember who it had been. The disaster of her broken engagement and the horror that had followed seemed to have left her deeply frightened of all strong feelings.

"You're still in that job with Orley Fitch, I suppose," she said to Helena over their coffee in Forte's, "or have you at last got around to leaving them? You're wasted there, you know. You could easily find something much more exciting."

"As a matter of fact," Helena said, "I've just made up my mind to leave them. Things have changed there recently and I can't stand the new set-up."

"Have you found another job yet?" Cleo asked.

"No, I haven't got as far as actually looking for anything," Helena answered. "But I've decided I'll have to. Old Mr. Fitch, whom I really loved, you know, died three months ago and I've been handed on to his son, who expects me to stand his whims, his incompetence, his stark laziness, and——" Her voice rose in indignation as she remembered what had happened that day. "*And* not to mind being *so* sweetly and *so* forgivingly blamed for all his own idiot mistakes. I won't take any more of it."

"But you haven't committed yourself to anything else yet," Cleo said.

"No," said Helena.

"So I suppose you just might like to spend a few months in Uyowa."

Cleo said it as if she were asking if Helena would like to go to a concert with her.

Groping among half-memories of half-read articles in newspapers, Helena said, "That's one of those African countries that's suddenly gone and changed its name, isn't it? You know, Africa's really the Dark Continent nowadays, as far as I'm concerned." She had not even started to take Cleo's proposition seriously. "I can't keep pace with all the new names of places, or who's in power. or what sort of system of government they're going in for at the moment, or even if they like us just now or hate us."

"If you'd go," Cleo said, "you'd be helping some friends of mine out of a very awkward jam. And you'd be staying in Tondolo—that's the capital, in case you don't know— which is a beautiful place with a marvellous climate and you'd be staying with awfully nice people. The Forrests, the people I stayed with when my parents died."

Cleo went straight on to tell Helena about the jam that the Forrests were in. Cleo's friends had a way of being in a jam. They seemed to specialise in it and Cleo was always ready to put herself out to help them. All that was wrong with this, from Helena's point of view, was that so often they didn't seem to be worth it. Usually she didn't much take to Cleo's friends. But who was Helena to criticise? Cleo had held out a helping hand to her too from time to time; at least had always listened with genuine attention to Helena's troubles of the moment. Just now Cleo was probably thinking as much of doing something nice for Helena as for these other friends of hers.

"Dennis Forrest is a lecturer in Economic History at London University," Cleo said. "You'll love him, Helena, you really will, he's got a quite extraordinary sort of charm. Odd, you know, but irresistible. And Marcia's an actress and good, really good, though she hasn't got very far yet. I'm not sure the trouble isn't that she's too good to go far, too subtle, you know. Anyway, she's tremendously intelligent and very good-looking in a weird, haggard sort of way. And Jean, who's seven, is a darling, though to be quite honest with you, she's a bit of a weirdie too. She isn't interested in anything in the world but animals. Human beings she can simply do without. But I should think that's because her home's been kind of lonely with her mother working. She's had to find compensations. Denis has done everything he possibly can for her, all the same, he's got his job to do too, and now there's this problem of some lectures he's been invited to give in America, and naturally he wants to go. You can't blame him for that, can you? I think myself it's very important for him to go on trying to make a very good thing of his career to make up for having a rather overpowering sort of wife like Marcia. So it seems that the obvious solution of the problem is to send Jean to his family in Tondolo for the three months he'll be away. They're longing to have her and they'll pay the fare and everything. Only you can't just send a seven-year-old girl all the way to Africa by herself, can you? So that's where you'd come in."

"But you can easily send a child off alone by air," Helena said. "You put her on board at one end in the charge of the stewardess and someone meets her at the other. It isn't like a train or a ship, where she can walk off, or fall off, or take up with strangers."

"Yes, but it's also when she's there, you see," Cleo said. "Denis's parents are pretty old, and it might be just a bit of a strain for them to look after her. Besides, they wouldn't be very thrilling company for her, though they're marvellous people, as I told you and enormously rich too. Mr. Forrest used just to be the headmaster of the mission school in Tondolo, but his wife always had loads of money and they live in a lovely house on one of the hills overlooking the town. It's cool and airy and it's got a wonderful garden. I often stayed there. I mean when I was a child, as well as when—well, you know about all that. I can remember Denis from those old days. Even then I simply loved him, though we were the wrong ages to take any real interest in one another. He's seven years older than I am, and when you're children that makes you practically different generations. I used to know his brother Paul much better. Paul's in Tondolo now, but I believe he's leaving and coming to England sometime soon. I don't know why. He's a doctor, and doctors here mostly want to go abroad, don't they, to make more money? But he's always been a contrary sort of character."

"But do your friends Denis and Marcia know what you're doing now?" Helena asked. "This asking me to look after Jean for them."

"No, they don't, actually," Cleo said. "They couldn't very well, when the idea of it only popped into my head when I saw you just now in the Underground. But I had dinner with Denis yesterday evening—Marcia's away in

Nottingham, acting in a super sort of Brechtish play at one of those funny little theatres down dark alleys—and he told me all about the problem."

"And it would be for three months?"

Unconsciously Cleo dropped her voice a little, as if she were telling Helena something confidential.

"My *own* guess is, Jean might stay for good. I think Denis would really like to get a job out there himself at Biriki College—that's the new university—and the old people would love to have him and Jean living near them. And Marcia would love it too, once she got there, though she's utterly against the idea now. But probably she could get up a progressive theatre club in Tondolo, or do something like that—I'm sure there are opportunities—and be very happy."

Just one thing was puzzling Helena.

"Cleo, you've always sounded as if you love the place yourself, so why don't you go? Are you in a job you can't leave?"

She knew that that was unlikely, jobs and men coming and going as easily as they did with Cleo.

"No," Cleo said. "Not really." She paused, frowning unhappily. "It's silly, but I still can't stand the idea of going back to that part of the world. Too many memories. Well, shall I phone Denis and see how he takes to the idea of sending you?"

"I don't know. I must think about it."

But only two days later Helena met Denis Forrest.

He telephoned in the morning and arranged to call at her flat at six o'clock that evening. He was punctual almost to the minute and came in muttering apologetically as he tried to stamp the soiled snow off his shoes. Snow had been falling for most of the day, and the streets were a grey, slippery mire. Helena offered him sherry. Accepting it, he went on to apologise for taking up her time; for imagining that she could possibly be interested in helping him out in his quandary; for everything that he could think of.

The odd thing was that at first Helena saw almost no sign of the charm that had captivated Cleo. He had a shy, solemn face, which was thin and white and far too narrow, so that although he had two quite good profiles, there did not seem to be enough space left between them to accommodate eyes, nose and mouth. It was only gradually, as he relaxed in the warmth of the gas fire, that the charm appeared. It was the kind that can belong to the naturally very shy when suddenly, for whatever reason, they succeed in convincing themselves that they are among friends, and all at once expand with boundless trustfulness. His pallid hatchet of a face became cheerful and expressive. His slight stammer disappeared.

"You know, I suppose, there's been a certain amount of political unpleasantness out there recently," he said. He had just let Helena refill his glass, then added absently, "Oh, I didn't mean to have any more. I drink too much, you know. It's something Marcia holds against me. And she's quite right, of course. It's a silly and perniciously expensive habit, particularly if you're trying to bring up a child. As I was saying though—what was I saying?—oh yes, about the unpleasantness in Uyowa. You do know all about it, don't you? Because you ought to, if you're going there, even though my parents wrote that our reports of the violence were ridiculously exaggerated."

Helena answered, "I did read something about it, I think, but I don't even try to keep up with African politics. Exactly what did happen?"

"The usual thing," he said, "an army coup. The president, Gilbert Kaggwa, whom I used to know quite well at one time and always thought unusually enlightened and honest as politicians go—well, he was nearly murdered and a few of his friends actually were, very nastily. But Kaggwa himself escaped somehow and he's in hiding somewhere; most people think out of the country, perhaps in Kenya. And the new president, put in by the army, is a man called Harvey Mukasa, who's fairly all right in himself, but his tribe's unpopular in the Tondolo region, where they're mostly still loyal to Kaggwa and might take it into their heads to hit back. So Mukasa's very frightened and practically never appears in public and simply does what the army tells him. The whites in the country haven't been much affected, although of course there's always a tendency to make us the scapegoats when there's any kind of trouble. The High Commissioner came in for a certain amount of abuse about nothing in particular, but seems to have ridden the storm, and there were a few random arrests and a journalist or two got kicked out of the country, but that's about all."

"I imagine if you were at all worried about any of it yourself, you wouldn't be sending Jean there," Helena said.

"Of course not. It's just that I shouldn't like to think you might have gone off without knowing all about it yourself."

"I don't think it sounds very frightening."

"Good. Then I think we ought to arrange that you and Jean should meet, because—well, she isn't . . ." He hesitated over the choice of just the right word to describe his daughter. "I don't think she's really a *difficult* child, you know. Anyway, I don't find her so. We understand each other pretty well. But I'm afraid she's a distinctly intolerant one. She likes you or she doesn't, and whichever it is, she isn't to be moved. I don't know where she gets it from—certainly not from me, because I find it quite difficult to make up my mind whether or not I really like people I've known half my life."

"Well, when shall we meet, Jean and I?" Helena asked.

"Saturday?" he suggested. "She won't have to go to school and Marcia'll be home this weekend. Perhaps we could all go to the zoo, if you don't dislike the idea. Jean's got a passion for animals, so it might help to create a favourable atmosphere."

"It sounds as if she's got you scared stiff," Helena said with a laugh.

"No, no, not at all. I told you, we understand each other pretty well." Then he laughed too. "All right, she has, but so have most people, and if I let her have her own way rather more than I should, it's because I think childhood's such a miserable period of one's life, even at the best of times."

"Was your own childhood miserable then?"

"Uns-p-peakable." His slight stammer came back as he said it.

"Then it seems odd, if you don't mind my saying so, that you're sending your daughter to the parents who made you so miserable," Helena said.

"Oh, good lord, it wasn't *their* fault," he said quickly. "I was always happy at home. But living out there, my brother and I had to be sent here to school in England, and God, how I hated that school! I was bored and cold and uncomfortable for six years and didn't learn anything. It's difficult for a child too, trying to live in two quite unrelated worlds. But my parents are the very nicest people imaginable. You'll like them immensely. I know I can absolutely count on that."

"Saturday, then," she said.

"Shall we call for you about two o'clock?" he suggested. "Then we can have tea in the zoo when we've been round the animals. Jean will enjoy that."

Helena agreed and he left. His second glass of sherry was only half-drunk. She wondered if she ought to have offered him something stronger.

But later she discovered that he was one of those people who never finish up anything. In the tea-room at the zoo his second cup of tea, his second scone were left after he had taken only a mouthful or two of each of them. He seemed to forget that Helena was there. His wife, after all, had not come. She had been detained in Nottingham over the weekend, he said, and all his attention was focused on his daughter. His eyes never left her and they were so bright with affection, his responses to everything she did were so quick and understanding, his sharing of her pleasure in elephants and camels, zebras and chimpanzees, was so simple and unforced that something in Helena was stirred curiously deeply. Her own father had never taken much interest in her. His passions were music, mathematics and golf and she did not happen to be talented at any one of them.

It had been just as they were about to go to the tea-room that Denis Forrest had suddenly asked her, "Miss Sebright, just why are you leaving the job you're in?"

It was almost the first question that he had asked her about herself. Till then he had appeared simply to take her at Cleo's valuation.

She did not want much to go into details. "I've been in it too long," she said.

"And that's the only reason?"

"Well, my old boss died and I don't much care for my new one."

"It isn't because you want to leave the country altogether?"

"I hadn't thought of it. No, I don't think so."

"Suppose you were offered some job while you were out there, would you feel inclined to take it?"

"I suppose it would depend on the job. But—no, that simply hadn't occurred to me."

"You see, we want our child brought home to us," he said. "We don't want to have to go and fetch her ourselves. Marcia and I are both pretty busy people."

"Then of course I'll bring her back, if that's part of the deal."

"Even if the job you were offered had great attractions—was well-paid, interesting—and you found yourself rather falling in love with the country? People do, you know, when they first get there."

"If it's part of the deal that I'm to bring Jean back, then I'll bring her back," said Helena.

"Good." He gave his warm, bright smile. "Of course, I knew we could rely on you, but I promised Marcia, when she rang up yesterday to say she couldn't come to-day, that I'd ask you those particular questions."

His eyes returned to entranced contemplation of his daughter.

Just then she was communing silently with a singularly hideous mandril. She had almost ignored Helena all the afternoon. But she had ignored her father too and a good many of the animals. She had particular friends among them and visited them in turn and gazed at them with an air of admiration and respect that was tinged with wistfulness, as if she knew that the day would never come when they would accept her as an equal. She was a small, sturdy child, with shaggy dark hair and a square, blunt-featured face which was quite attractive when her interest was aroused, yet had a disturbing, unchildlike quality about it. She could hardly have been less like her father.

The next morning Denis Forrest rang Helena up to tell her that Jean had liked her enormously.

"Did she?" Helena said. "She didn't show it much."

"She never does. But she wouldn't have said it if she didn't meant it. She doesn't do that either. So you'll go, won't you? It's settled?"

"Yes—oh yes! And—thank you so much—it's so very good of you!" Suddenly all the excitement that Helena had been trying to keep in check in case the whole thing fell through came bursting out of her. "I'm looking forward to is so much. It's so good of you to pick on me."

As if her little explosion embarrassed him, he began to stammer again. "I hope you'll st-still think so when you get there. I hope you won't find you've t-taken on rather more than you've bargained for. I ought to warn you, I suppose, Jean's got one rather awkward habit. She suddenly gets some odd notion into her head and off she goes. The first time it was to find the North Pole. God knows what she thought the North Pole was—a sort of painted maypole, I think, stuck into the ground somewhere in North London. Anyway, she packed her pyjamas and her teddy-bear into a shoe-box and set off. Luckily she only got as far as the end of the road when her courage failed her. A neighbour described it to us. She gave a shriek and dropped the shoe-box and came running home."

"How old was she then?" Helena asked.

"Only four. But she's done the same sort of thing once or twice since then, rather more successfully. Once we were so frantic we had the police out looking for her and they found her riding round and round London on the Underground. And it's nothing for her to slip off by herself to feed the pigeons in Trafalgar Square."

"So part of my job is to be a watch-dog."

"Well, sort of. But I'm sure she won't give you any real trouble. She only does that sort of thing when she's bored or unhappy, and that couldn't possibly happen in Tondolo. Now about arrangements. You've got a passport, I expect, but you'll need an entry permit and smallpox vaccination and inoculation against yellow fever. . . ."

They went on to discuss the details of the journey.

And now it was almost over. . . .

Waking abruptly from a short, uneasy sleep, Helena was aware of strange coloured lights and a roaring in her ears. She did not understand what was happening. She could not remember where she was and suddenly she was cold with fear. But almost at once this feeling faded, for the roaring was only the steady drone of a VC10, flying at forty thousand feet above the earth, and the lights were the dawn. There was a broad band of flame along the horizon where the froth of cloud below the plane ended, and above that a shimmering of pale yellow that merged into green, and above that blue, which grew brighter and richer with every moment, while over everything there was a veil of pale lavender shadow, the last faint trace of the darkness.

A moment later the veil was twitched aside and vanished. Everything was ablaze. Helena wriggled in her narrow seat, massaged her neck, which was stiff from the awkwardness of the position in which she had fallen asleep, and combed her fingers through her short, fair hair. Yawning, she groped with her toes for the shoes that she had kicked off in the night. Still looking out at the dawn, she saw the clouds thin away and from far below a face looking up at her. That was how it struck her. The oldest face in the world, grey, wrinkled, empty of meaning.

In dreamy astonishment she said to herself, "It's the Sahara—Africa!"

She was filled now with excitement, a happy, heady response to the strangeness of being there, looking down at the first desert that she had ever seen in her life. It was no longer a face. There was too much of it. It was a sea. Those wrinkles were waves; waves that never moved; still, carven ridges, just as the waves of the real sea seem to be when you look down at them from forty thousand feet. Only these waves had no glitter, no blue radiance. They were the colour of death.

A road, ruled unbelievably straight across that lifeless sea of rock and sand, was itself a reminder of death. For of course it was a military road, built during the war that had been fought down there when Helena was an infant in arms. Or perhaps it had been during some other war. Besides being the most notable breeding ground of religions in the world, this desert must be about its direst battlefield. One bloody campaign after another had been fought in its vastness. Yet here was Helena, aged twenty-six, in general fairly inexperienced, and, when it came to geography, quite shockingly ignorant, gliding smoothly across the great pale expanse with no more discomfort than a slight crick in the neck and a faint feeling that she was missing something.

But air-travel always gave her the feeling of missing something. It gave too much and too little all at the same time, with the result that, except for occasional moments of drama, like the dawn, it was really pretty boring.

She was already beginning to be bored by the desert, which threatened, she realised, to go on unchangingly for a very long time. Turning away from it, she looked at the child, curled up, sound asleep, on the two seats beside her. Jean Forrest's rosy face looked peacefully relaxed above the airline rug with which Helena had covered her in the night. It didn't seem to worry Jean much, being pushed here and there like a piece of furniture that didn't quite fit in anywhere, that was always just a little bit in the way. Helena felt a pang of pity for her, half-wishing suddenly that she had not got herself involved in the Forrests' affairs. Yet who wouldn't have jumped at the chance to go to Africa? To Uyowa? To Tondolo? Actually to be paid for going?

Helena was always inclined to jump at chances, to leap first and look later. And usually a good while later and even then not very carefully. So she had not learnt as much as she might have from experience.

CHAPTER II

The desert below had given way to a scrubby sort of vegetation, sparse and brown. From the height at which the plane was flying, Helena could not tell if this consisted of tall trees or of little bushes. Then suddenly in the midst of the arid country she saw a rectangle of emerald green. It was a plantation of some sort, with a house in the middle of it. It seemed absurd, at that height, to feel gladness at the mere sight of a human habitation, yet for a moment she had an inkling of how a traveller down there in the dust and the heat must feel on coming to such a place, receiving reassurance that there was still life on earth.

A few minutes later life also began to stir in the plane. Stewardesses appeared with breakfast trays. Helena nudged Jean awake.

She woke completely all at once, like a young animal, and sat up with a swift, eager movement.

"Are we nearly there?" she asked.

"It won't be long now."

"Shall I change my dress, then? Only it doesn't feel very hot yet." She was wearing a warm yellow woollen pullover and a short tartan skirt.

"I expect it'll be hot enough when we get out of the plane," Helena said. "But let's have breakfast first, since they're bringing it, then there'll still be time to wash and change."

"All right. I hope it's a good breakfast. I'm hungry."

Fairly continuous hunger, Helena had noticed, was another characteristic that Jean shared with the animal kingdom.

When breakfast came, she ate with speed and concentration, as she did most things. She gave Helena the feeling of having a tremendous amount of energy stored up in her small, compact body. An unusual amount of intelligence too, behind her inexpressive features. But Helena had not had much experience of children. She was the youngest in her own family and had never had to cope with younger brothers and sisters, and now, although the elder ones were all married, none of them had yet produced any nieces or nephews for her to practise on.

She felt rather helpless in her relationship with Jean Forrest. If the child were to assert herself in some unexpected way, she would not have the faintest idea how to cope with it. Almost diffidently she said presently, "Perhaps you'd better change now, Jean."

"All right." This was Jean's good-humoured response to a lot of things that were said to her, which it had been a relief to Helena to discover.

Pulling their overnight bag out from under the seat, she took out a cotton dress for Jean, and Jean disappeared with it to the toilet. Helena herself did not change. She only took off the jacket that she had worn through the night and bundled it into the bag, tied a scarf round her hair and took her sun-glasses out of her handbag.

She was impatient to arrive now, longing for a bath and hoping that on arrival someone would offer her some stronger coffee than the airline stuff. But of course, in Uyowa they were four hours ahead of London. It would be almost lunch-time when the plane landed. She altered her watch.

At her elbow Jean's composed voice observed, "I suppose we shan't actually see an elephant to-day, shall we? Or a giraffe or anything?"

"You'll see your grandparents," Helena said. "I'm sorry they're only people."

"Yes, but it's true, isn't it—I shall see lots of animals? Daddy promised." Jean's eyes, those of the utterly single-minded, gazed deeply into Helena's.

The look made Helena wonder suddenly how often this child had been promised things that had never materialised, how much disappointment was a normal part of her life. But how could you help failing someone so dedicated? At that moment it struck Helena that for almost the first time in her life, she was responsible for another person, and, as it happened, not an ordinary person. All that desperate earnestness in Jean, which at present was directed towards elephants and giraffes, what might it not be in ten years' time? In twenty? If things went as they should with her, what might she not become? And for the present it was Helena's responsibility to see that things did go as they should.

The plane was going down steeply now. Seat belts had been fastened. Red roofs showed among green trees and a few minutes later the wheels of the plane bounced on the runway at Igambo, the airport for Tondolo. Helena and Jean emerged into heat and sunlight.

A slender young woman waiting at the foot of the steps asked them, "Do you require transport?"

She had skin the colour of bitter chocolate, a pale khaki cotton dress and a perky little leopard skin cap on her kinky black hair.

"Thank you, I think we're being met," Helena answered.

She and Jean walked towards the airport buildings.

The heat seemed to be coming up at them out of the ground. It could hardly be coming from a sky so softly, remotely blue, on which the few great motionless clouds looked like massive groups of sculpture. Clustered behind some railings a group of Indian women were waiting to meet someone who had arrived on the plane. The vivid colours of their saris made it look as if the railings were garlanded with brilliant flowers. Jean's hand slid into Helena's and held it rather tightly. Their passports were examined by a short, portly man in an open-necked white shirt and dark trousers. He wished them a pleasant holiday in Uyowa, then another man looked at their suitcases and chalked them without asking them to open them. Helena looked round, hoping that she had been right that someone would be there to meet them.

But instantly she became interested in the unfamiliarity of the scene around her, imposed, as it was, on the international uniformity of airports; unfamiliarity which came from dark faces and unknown languages, mingling with the ubiquitous English. The thin, angular African men, almost all dressed in white shirts and narrow black trousers, were as quiet in their movements as shadows. The plumper

Indians, mostly in large family groups, exclaimed noisily and greeted and embraced one another demonstratively. The few whites looked flustered and impatient and too hot. And somehow, in spite of everything, uniformity won. Airports are basically the same everywhere. Helena saw that she would have to wait until she was clear of coffee lounges and bars and information desks and the incomprehensible sounds that came bellowing out of the loudspeakers before she could begin to take in the fact that she was in Africa.

A white man in shorts and an open-necked shirt came thrusting through the crowd towards her and Jean and said, "Miss Sebright? I'm Paul Forrest."

He did not look flustered or impatient or too hot, but completely accustomed to his surroundings and at the same time detached from them; also, so like Jean that it had hardly been necessary for him to introduce himself. He had her square, blunt-featured face, her rough dark hair, her sturdy build. Until then Helena had assumed that Jean, being so unlike her father, must resemble her mother, but now it seemed plain that it was she who was a typical Forrest and Denis who had diverged from the family pattern.

Paul Forrest was of medium height, lightly built but with broad, muscular shoulders and a neat, poised energy in his movements. He had a fairly pleasant, if cool, smile and an unusually direct gaze. It was odd, therefore, that Helena's first impression of him was that he was hostile to her. For some reason, she felt, he had decided on sight, or perhaps even before that, that he had no use for her. He gave her the sense that he regarded her rather like a piece of luggage that he had been sent to collect and which he knew would be full of utterly unwanted things. But there was not much more enthusiasm in his expression when he turned to Jean.

She held out her hand to him and said cautiously, "How do you do?"

"How do you do?" he responded, almost as cautiously. They were so alike in their noncommittal appraisal of one another that it was almost comic.

"The car's outside," he said. "Is this all your luggage, Miss Sebright?"

Helena said that it was and he signalled to a porter. As they followed the man to the car, Paul Forrest asked the usual questions, had they had a good journey, what was the weather like in London, how were Denis and Marcia? But he did not sound much interested in the answers. Jean, walking between him and Helena, looked at the ground. It was impossible to tell from the child's face what opinion she had formed of her uncle.

She sat beside him in the car and Helena took the back seat. Paul drove fast along the good, broad road to Tondolo, which was almost empty of traffic, except for the occasional Mercedes that came swooping past them, horn blaring, and filled to the brim with Indians. He made one or two attempts to talk to Jean, but she had retired into the depths of one of her silences, staring steadily at the road ahead of her and simply not replying.

"Unnerving," he observed to Helena presently. "Tiredness, is it, or has she taken an acute dislike to me?"

Helena disapproved very much of talking about children to their faces as if they were not there, but she answered, "Perhaps she thinks you've taken a dislike to her."

"Why ever should she?"

"She may have been all set for a—well, a rather more effusive greeting."

"But we hardly know each other," he said. "Don't know each other at all, really. Actually I haven't seen her since I was last in England and that's about four years ago. You don't remember that, do you, Jean?"

Without speaking, she gave a very faint shake of her head.

"There you are," he said.

"I believe you're going home again soon, aren't you?" Helena said it merely to say something. The unfamiliarity that she had failed to find in the airport at Igambo had engulfed her now and, tired as she was, was submerging her consciousness in a kind of glowing dream. The road to Tondolo wound through flat, sparsely wooded country and every bush, every tree was different from any that she had ever seen before. Even the grass growing by the roadside was a different kind of grass from any that she knew.

"Home?" Paul Forrest said. "I'd say I was leaving it. I was born here, you know. I grew up here."

"Then why are you leaving? Don't they need doctors here?"

"Don't they need them in Britain too? I've been told you do."

She did not answer because she was gazing raptly at a tree about the size of a large wild cherry, with flowers of a flame-colour so brilliant that they looked like a small, creeping fire, consuming the whole tree. The earth was a harsh, vivid red. Here and there it had been strangely piled up in tall cones, some of them six feet high. Ant-hills, she guessed. Among the ant-hills and the trees there were dwellings, small huts, some of them round, with pointed, thatched roofs, some of them crumbling shacks with roofs of corrugated iron or anything else that could be used to patch them up, and all of them so little, so low, that it would have been quite easy to miss them and mistake a teeming countryside for empty bush.

Suddenly Jean screamed at the top of her voice.

The car swerved sharply. Paul swore wildly. Then, as he regained control of the car and of himself, he said, "God, don't ever do that again, Jean! You nearly had us in the ditch."

"But the dog there—you were going to run over it!" she cried.

"I wasn't. But it was dead already, wasn't it? Never risk the lives of three live human beings for the sake of one dead dog."

"Suppose it wasn't dead!" she said shrilly.

"It was, Jean," Helena said. She had caught a glimpse of a mangy-looking brown dog lying in the middle of the road. The creature could not have been anything but dead, and for some time too.

"Then why doesn't somebody bury it?" Jean demanded.

"That's something no one in his senses would think

of doing," Paul replied. "Much too dangerous, I assure you."

"Why? Because of disease of some sort?" Helena asked.

"Something much worse than disease," he said. "A spell. You see, if someone puts a spell on you, one of the ways you can get rid of it is to kill a dog, put it in the road and scatter pennies over it. Then everyone who comes along and helps himself to a penny or two will get a small, relatively harmless dose of the spell, and gradually it'll be drawn off you. But if anyone moved the dog itself, God knows what would happen to him, besides, of course, defeating the whole object of the exercise."

"Then do many people here still believe in magic?" Helena asked.

"You'd be astonished how many," he said. "White magic and black. You have to understand that, as they see it, there's no such thing as, for instance, a natural death. Nothing that happens is natural. There's intention behind everything. But at the same time you'd be astonished at how much of it makes sense of a sort. Some of it's just sound psychology, but there are chemical firms pouring thousands of pounds into trying to find out how some of the witch doctors' herbal remedies work."

"I don't believe in magic," Jean stated abruptly.

"I don't either, Jean," he answered seriously, for which only Helena gave him a good mark. "All the same, it's extraordinary how believing enough in a thing can make it work."

"Please," Jean went on, almost loquaciously, now that the ice had been broken, "when shall I see some more animals—live ones?"

"When we go to the Game Reserves," he said. "You'll see plenty then."

"When will we go?"

"Soon. As soon as we can manage. Is that what you're interested in—animals?"

"Yes, I'm *very* interested indeed," she answered at her most grown-up.

"Then we must fix something up for you as quickly as possible, mustn't we? Meanwhile, there's a dog at home, a puppy. He's a cross-breed between a Border collie and a French bouvier, and he's called Bongo. Do you care for dogs?"

She took a moment to answer, then breathed a hushed, "Yes," as if the happiness of having a dog in the house were almost too much for her.

A minute or two later they were entering Tondolo.

Helena's first impression of the town was of a glowing riot of colour. Everywhere there were jacarandas, cassias, frangipanni, hibiscus and bougainvillaea, red, pink, purple, white and tawny orange. There were trees covered in great purple clumps of what looked like immense potato flowers. There were beds of roses. Standing among the flowers there were some good plain modern buildings, white and clean-looking. There were streets of attractive shops.

"Why, it's beautiful!" Helena exclaimed.

"Some of it isn't," Paul Forrest said. "Nor are some of the things that happen here."

"Is that why you're leaving?"

"Do you mean, am I scared?" he asked bluntly. "Not at the moment. I'm used to the things that go on and the recent troubles seem to have quietened down. But I don't think there's any future here for people like me and the conditions of work are unspeakably frustrating. You can't get the standard of assistants you need. You can't get the equipment. If I had a saintly temperament it might be different, but I haven't. I'm even rather short of normal patience."

"Where did you train?" Helena asked.

"At Edinburgh," he said.

"But you said you grew up out here."

"So I did, except for school and university."

"That's quite a big exception."

"Yes, big enough to be very unsettling. That's one of the prices of empire, you know. It's produced in its time an awful lot of badly unsettled people. I'm one of those. I don't know where I belong. But perhaps you're the same, or why have you come out here?"

"I came because I thought I'd never have another chance

like it." She broke off as he slowed the car down to let two women cross the road. They were both splendidly massive, high-breasted, slow-moving. They had bright-coloured scarves tied round their heads and wore long, full-skirted dresses, which looked as if their original inspiration might have been one belonging to some Edwardian missionary's wife, except that they were in coloured prints in which no missionary's wife would have dared to be seen, orange and pink and emerald and sapphire. Against those bitter chocolate skins they looked like royal robes. Both women walked like queens.

"Beautiful!" Helena exclaimed again, as the car went on up a winding road that climbed one of the low hills overlooking the town, and a few minutes later turned in at the gate of a pleasant-looking white house, set in a big, perfectly kept garden.

An elderly man and woman, who had plainly been waiting and watching for this moment on the verandah, came to meet them, accompanied by a huge, bounding puppy. The woman was short and stocky and about sixty, powerfully but trimly built and dressed in a red shirt, black slacks and sandals. She had short grey hair, a deeply tanned face, a very straight back and the blunt nose and strong chin that she had handed on to her younger son and her granddaughter. Her husband looked a good deal older than she was. He was a slender wisp of a man, at a first glance fragile, yet when you looked more carefully, Helena saw, you realised that he was full of wonderful energy for a man of at least seventy. There was still springiness in all his movements. They were quick and sure. His light blue eyes were very bright and lively.

Both the Forrests lavished kisses and embraces on Jean, in which the puppy tried to share, then they turned to Helena.

"It's so good of you to come here to help us," Mrs. Forrest said, giving her a firm handshake. "It's so lucky for us you were able to arrange it."

From the warmth of her tone, it could easily have been thought that she really was unaware that all the goodness in the arrangements made between them and Helena had been on their side, and all the luck on hers, escaping, as she had, from a London February to this sunny, flowery paradise.

Mrs. Forrest put one arm through Jean's and one through Helena's and took them towards the house.

"You'll want baths, both of you," she said. "Helena—I shall call you Helena—you'll want to unpack and change into something cool. Lunch is in about an hour's time, so don't hurry. But you'd like a drink first, of course. I'll send it up to your room. Gin? Whisky? Or just something long and cool? Orange squash? Our own, it doesn't come out of a bottle."

She chatted on, taking them on to the verandah of the white house, into a big, shady sitting-room, up a flight of stairs and to their bedrooms, which were side by side, each with a bathroom opening out of it. All the walls in the house were white; the floors were of polished woodblocks; there was very little furniture and what there was was very simple, but made of unusual and attractive woods. All the colour in the house came from a few paintings on the walls and the bowls of flowers everywhere.

A smiling young man in a garment like a long white night-shirt, who had greeted Jean and Helena on the verandah by taking a hand of each between both of his, brought their luggage up to their rooms and left them. Helena's room had a balcony. As soon as she was alone she went out on to it and looked round. A creeper with polished, laurel-like leaves and flowers like enormous buttercups was twined round the railing. The sun was directly overhead in the deceptively pallid sky. The shadows under the trees in the garden were dark and small. There were other houses on the hillside, white, with red roofs, standing among green lawns, shaded by eucalyptus trees and a few palms. Everything was modern, luxurious, charming. It was difficult to realise that it was in the same world as those hovels among the anthills, with the dead dog in the road.

Helena had a nice, deep, tepid bath and when she came out of it found a tall glass of iced orange squash waiting on her dressing-table. She sipped it slowly, then dressed slowly, putting on a short white skirt, a sleeveless pink and white striped blouse and white sandals. Her bare legs were much too pale to please her, but they always were. She had the sort of fair skin that never takes on a satisfactory tan.

Going downstairs, she found the Forrests waiting for her to go in to lunch, a meal which, she was a little disconcerted to find, since it was her first meal in Africa, consisted of roast beef and Yorkshire pudding. It was served by more than one servant, she was fairly sure of that, but as they dressed identically in that long, white garment like a nightshirt, and as to her inexperienced eyes all their round dark faces still looked alike, she could not really have said how many quietly came and went through the door from the kitchen.

After lunch Mrs. Forrest said, "You and Jean will want to sleep now."

She had a habit, Helena realised, of telling people what they wanted and then of very kindly seeing that they got it. Obediently, she and Jean went up to their rooms, and Helena, as she had been told to, soon fell asleep.

When she woke the sun was low, though it was not yet dusk. The air was cooler. She put on one of her better cotton dresses and high-heeled sandals and went downstairs. She found Mr. and Mrs. Forrest on the verandah. Mrs. Forrest had changed into a sleeveless dress of brightly patterned silk, the bold colours of which suited her strong features and tanned skin. Mr. Forrest had on a different shirt from the morning and his white hair was slicked back after a recent bath. Jean and Paul Forrest were playing with the puppy, Bongo, on the lawn, throwing a ball for him and trying to teach him to bring it back. When Bongo teased Paul by dropping the ball at his feet, then racing away with it again before he could pick it up, even though he moved with astonishing speed, Jean screamed with laughter. They seemed quite to have got over their reserve with one another. Paul's rather hard face had come youthfully alive and Jean looked happier and more normally childish than Helena had yet seen her.

Watching them contentedly as Mr. Forrest gave Helena a drink, Mrs. Forrest said, "It'll be so good for Jean, staying here. You can see she needs sunshine and fresh air. A flat in London is no place for a child. And with her mother away half the time, what a situation! Of course, you've met my daughter-in-law, Marcia, Helena?"

"No," Helena said. "As a matter of fact, she was away, acting in something in Nottingham."

"Ah," Mrs. Forrest said and gave Helena an intent look that puzzled her slightly. "And Denis was doing his own cooking and looking after Jean, I suppose, perhaps even without the help of some awful, unreliable charwoman. Could anything be more ridiculous? I've told Denis, I don't know how often, that he'd be far better off here. He can get a job at Biriki—I know he can, he can have one for the asking—and he could have a nice house and servants and live like a civilised person. But he's always let Marcia bully him, and she talks about her career, and seems to think too that we're all in danger of being beaten up or murdered at any moment. She simply doesn't understand the situation. Of course the people blow up from time to time and murder a good many of one another. Naturally. Anyone who's known them all her life, as I have, could have told you that was bound to happen as soon as they got independence. You can't create a nation out of a lot of tribes who've hated each other for hundreds of years and then expect them to live at peace. But they've nothing against us now. Do you know, there are actually more whites employed in Uyowa than there were before independence? There's no doubt at all in my mind that a man like Denis could settle here and be very happy."

"We'd be very happy to have him here—isn't that what you mean?" Mr. Forrest's gentle voice sounded almost exactly like Denis's, except that he had no stammer. "But I don't believe an actress of any quality—and we've been told, haven't we, that Marcia's talented?—can give up her career like giving away an old dress. Acting is one of those built-in things that can't be shed overnight."

"Well, she should make the effort for the sake of her

husband and child—if she wants to keep them," his wife said.

"But Denis may really not wish to come," Mr. Forrest went on. "After all this time in London he's probably set his sights far higher than Biriki."

Mrs. Forrest shook her head. "He'd love to come home. I know my Denis. He's just let himself be bullied into staying in England by that awful woman. Paul, now—I wish I felt so sure I understood what's going on in him. This going to England—is it really because he's dissatisfied here, or is it simply that he's still in love with Cleo Grant and hoping she'll listen to him at last? I've a sort of feeling that's what's really behind it. Anyway, that's something I can understand. The reasons he gives himself for going seem to me complete nonsense." She turned to Helena. "You know Cleo Grant, don't you? How is she? Her parents were great friends of ours, you know, and I used to think at one time that she and Paul were going to marry. But she went and fell in love with some awful Jugoslav."

"Czech," her husband said.

"Czech, Jugoslav, Rumanian. . . ." She shrugged her shoulders. "The moment I heard about it, I knew it would end in disaster. I told Cleo so. I said, 'My dear,'—I'm very fond of her, you know—I said, 'My dear, you're making the mistake of your life. You and he have totally different backgrounds, you'll never be happy.' But the poor girl wouldn't listen to me."

"I've often wondered what happened to the man," Mr. Forrest said. "The last we heard of him, he'd an agency of some sort in the Congo."

"Cleo can be glad she's out of that, anyway," Mrs. Forrest said. "Now, Helena, how would you like a stroll round the garden with my husband? He's building a pergola and he's dying to show it off to you as well as tell you all about any plants you don't know. Off you go, both of you, before it gets dark."

Unresistingly doing as they were told, Mr. Forrest and Helena got up and went down the steps from the verandah.

As they started to walk slowly round the garden together,

Jean came racing up to them, with Bongo bounding at her side.

"Isn't he *lovely*, Helena?" she panted and actually threw her arms round Helena's waist for a moment in her first display of affection. "Do you know why he nips people's ankles? Paul says it's because he's a sheep dog and he thinks we're all sheep."

She and the puppy ran off again.

"Paul seems to have found the way to her heart—and she to his." Mr. Forrest sighed. "We're going to miss him. He leaves at the end of next week. I hope he knows what he's doing, returning to England. I believe he'll have to work far harder than here, and for less money. He was building up a good practice in Tondolo, but in England he's only going to be an assistant in a group practice, with the hope that he'll be taken into partnership later if they like him."

"Have you always lived in Tondolo yourself?" Helena asked him.

"Goodness me, no," Mr. Forrest answered. "I grew up in Millyham—that's a village a few miles from Tunbridge Wells. You don't know it, by any chance?"

"I'm afraid I don't."

"But you know the kind of place, a church, a vicarage, a pub, a dozen cottages, a few farms. My father was the vicar. And I still have a sort of dream of ending my days there, or somewhere like it, only I'm afraid my wife wouldn't care for it much. I wonder if it's a great deal changed. Been built-up, you know, housing estates and that sort of thing. It was really very lovely when I was a child, though I didn't appreciate it. All I wanted was to travel and see the world, and although of course I've been back to England a number of times, it's generally been to London, or visiting friends in different parts of the country, or fishing in Scotland. . . . Now look at this. Have you ever seen a pau-pau before?"

They had been strolling on across the lawn, which was baked dry from lack of rain, with fissures in the red earth seaming the brownish grass. Mr. Forrest had stopped to

B

point out a tree with a slender trunk and a tuft of feathery leaves at the top.

"You'll have some pau-pau for breakfast, I expect," he said. "And these you may know, even if you've never seen them growing out of doors before." He pointed to a great patch of scarlet amaryllis. "They grow here like weeds. And that's a gardenia, of course. And here's my pergola. . . ." He stood still, looking at the stumps of three pillars, each about two feet high, that stuck up out of a bare patch of earth. "That *was* my pergola yesterday. Dear, dear, it's fallen down again."

A young man, dressed in shorts and a singlet, who had a strikingly vivid, dark face and a thin, lithe body, was collecting the fallen bricks, scattered around the pillars. Looking up at Mr. Forrest with a broad smile, he said in a tone of immense satisfaction, "Yes, *bwana*, they fall down."

"I haven't really learnt the art of building yet, have I, Wilbraham?" Mr. Forrest said.

"Not yet, *bwana*, but you learn. Better next time."

"I hope so. Wilbraham, this is Miss Sebright, who's come to stay with us. She comes from London."

Wilbraham flashed his bright grin at Helena and went on picking up the bricks.

As Helena and Mr. Forrest walked away again, he said, "That's the third time they've fallen down, you know. I thought at first it was because I'd tried making them too thin, so I added an extra course. Then, when they fell down again, I thought I must have put too much sand in with the cement. This time, for all I know, I put too little. And I was half-expecting them to topple, because when I examined them this morning, they swayed. They distinctly swayed. Yet I only pushed at them quite gently. Perhaps I ought to have dug deeper foundations. I think I must get advice from someone who really understands these matters. Wilbraham's delighted, of course, at finding me so incompetent. He's a nice fellow. Very nice. An excellent gardener and a very hard worker. Even my wife approves of him and she's very hard to please. She's convinced all the servants stop working the moment she takes her eye off them. But he does enjoy it when I make a fool of myself."

"What are you going to grow over the pergola?" Helena asked.

"I'm not sure. Roses, perhaps. I remember a rose pergola we had at home. . . . But I might plant dutchman's pipes or an allamanda. The main thing is, it gives me something to do. I need some practical occupation, now that I've retired."

In the last few minutes, with astonishing suddenness, the light had gone. There had been a brief, purple-tinged twilight, then darkness. Jean and Paul Forrest had gone into the house, but Bongo was still on the prowl. So was a dark figure, who suddenly emerged, soft-footed, from behind a tree. He was carrying a rifle.

"Good evening, *bwana*," he said.

"Good evening, Malcolm," Mr. Forrest replied and as he and Helena went into the house, explained, "The night watchman."

"Does he always carry a gun?" she asked.

"Oh yes, though I couldn't say for certain if he knows how to use it. But it would probably make him feel brave if he had to cope with a prowler. Now come and finish your drink, then I expect it'll be time for dinner."

They joined Mrs. Forrest and Paul on the verandah.

The animation that had made Paul attractive while he had been playing with Jean had gone. He had again become the self-contained, rather prickly person who had met Jean and Helena at the airport. Jean, Mrs. Forrest said, had already gone to bed. She had just gone up to say good night to her and had found her sound asleep already.

"And you," she said to Helena, "will want to go to bed soon. We all generally go to bed early and get up early. But you must sleep as late as you like to-morrow. You're probably tired from the sudden change of temperature, coming from England, and you may find you're affected by the altitude too. Many people are at first, though of course it's what makes the climate here so delightful. So sleep as late as you like and don't come down till you want to."

But next morning Helena was not allowed to sleep late.

It was still dark when Mrs. Forrest, in a crimson dressing-gown and with her grey hair tumbled, came running into the room and shook Helena awake.

"There's a battle going on in the town," she said. "There's mortar and rifle fire. Paul's gone up to the top of the hill in the car to see if he can make out what's going on. And I'm going to make some tea. Come down if you want some."

CHAPTER III

Helena sat up, bleary-eyed. She could hear firing faintly in the distance. Mrs. Forrest had gone already. Getting up, Helena put on her dressing-gown and went downstairs. Except for the night-watchman, who was standing in the gateway, none of the servants was about. They had their own quarters, built out as a wing of the house, and either had not been wakened by the firing or had decided not to emerge. Mrs. Forrest was in the kitchen, slamming cups and saucers on to a tray. Her movements were more violent than usual, but that was the only sign she gave of nervousness. Helena was not yet scared, but that was because she had not begun to take in what was happening.

As they stood there in the kitchen, the firing stopped. At the same time the darkness began to go. It went as quickly as it had come. It was almost as if a great screen had been hurriedly folded up and put away, revealing that really the daylight had been there all along, only temporarily hidden. For a few minutes there was a lovely lavender tint to the light, then that disappeared. The kettle began to hum. It took no longer for the darkness to change to daylight than for Mrs. Forrest to make the tea.

Helena had not been able to help her because she had not known where to look for the tea or the sugar or anything else. But watching Mrs. Forrest, Helena had had an incongruous thought. Look at the two of us, she had thought, in this lovely modern kitchen, all white and primrose yellow; look at the sink unit and the refrigerator and the electric stove; look at all the built-in cupboards. A housewife's dream! And only a hundred years ago or thereabouts, Livingstone—or was it Speke or Grant or Stanley?—passed this way. Why, one of them might have camped on this very spot. And think of all they endured then, the fearful hardships, the disease, the dangers. It's been too fast, she thought. Things can't change as fast as this. It's expecting too much.

37

But danger at least was still there, though it had gone silent for the moment. Helena did not like the silence. She preferred the firing. As long as she could hear it she could go on assuring herself that it was really quite a long way off.

"We'll have tea on the verandah," Mrs. Forrest said and went briskly out, carrying the tray. "It rather sounds as if it's all over, whatever it was. Last time, when they tried to kill Kaggwa, there was a lot more noise, and it lasted much longer."

"What did you do?" Helena asked.

"Oh, we just stayed here and didn't go out much for a few days."

"And that was all?"

"What else was there to do? It was no concern of ours— though we always liked and admired poor Kaggwa. He was a pupil of my husband's, you know, in the old mission school days. Hugh spotted his talents when he was quite a child, and we've always thought he was by far the best man they've got here. Sugar?"

"No, thank you." They had sat down on the cane chairs. "He's still supposed to be alive, isn't he?"

"So it's said. But he may have been quietly murdered and shovelled out of sight. You never know."

The words were cold-blooded. But Helena had the feeling that this was simply the way in which Mrs. Forrest expressed fear, controlled it, did her best to turn it into courage. She was naturally a very warm-hearted person, Helena thought; domineering, of course, and perhaps over-possessive, but still kind, generous and not at all callous.

Helena's own fear was beginning to emerge as irritability. When Bongo came bounding in from the garden and jumped all over her, licking her face and digging his claws into her through her thin dressing-gown, she pushed him away with a violence that took her as well as the puppy by surprise. He retired a yard or two, looked at her with hurt incredulity, forgave her, and came lunging at her again. She controlled herself this time and put her arms round him, at which he started messily licking her face.

Mr. Forrest came up on to the verandah after Bongo. He had been walking round the garden. Like his wife and Helena, he was in a dressing-gown.

"Goodness me, Judy," he said to his wife when he saw Helena, "don't tell me you woke the poor girl! What a thing to do. After that journey she ought to have had a chance to catch up on her sleep."

"I thought she might prefer not to miss everything." There was irony in Mrs. Forrest's voice as she poured out a cup of tea for him.

"There was nothing to miss." He took his tea and stood, drinking it, looking towards the town. "At least you didn't wake Jean?"

"Of course not."

"Though I imagine she's the one who'd be most sorry at missing anything that was going on. Really I'm very sorry you've been disturbed, Helena. Why don't you go back to bed?"

She did not know him well enough to be able to judge whether his calm was genuine or not. It seemed to her that it was, that his lined yet youthful face was concealing nothing.

She answered, "I don't think I want to. I'm quite wide awake now."

There was a short silence, during which they all listened.

Suddenly she became aware that the silence was not silence at all. The garden was full of birds singing. They sang sweet, unfamiliar songs, while a very elegantly shaped bird with plumage the colour of gun-metal, brightened with flashes of blue, came to settle on a bush near the verandah and preen itself.

After a little while Mrs. Forrest said, "I don't think it *can* have been anything."

"I was just out taking a look at my poor pergola," Mr. Forrest remarked as if he thought it was more than time to drop a tiresome subject, "and I've been deciding the trouble is I haven't been taking it seriously enough. Building isn't easy and I've been acting as if it were. That's been my mistake. I must get down to fundamentals."

"That lovely bird," Helena said, pointing at the bush, "what is it?"

"A starling," Mr. Forrest replied. "Not much like the flat-footed things you have at home, is it? Are you interested in birds? If you are, I've got a very useful book——"

"Hugh! Hugh!" Mrs. Forrest began to laugh wildly, with hysteria in the sound. She turned to Helena. "I've never been able to decide if it helps or not, the way he simply won't take anything seriously. Because that's what it is, you know. You can call it a stiff upper lip if you want to, but down underneath he simply doesn't *mind* what happens. He can always make me feel a fool for getting excited. But sometimes I'm sure it's right to get excited. I'm sure one shouldn't simply sit back and wait. . . . Ah, here's Paul."

She sounded as if she expected more genuine reassurance from her son than from her husband.

The car had just turned in at the gate. Paul got out and came up on to the verandah, brisk, efficient-looking, but tenser than he probably wished to appear.

"I don't know what it was," he said. "It was down round the barracks. There were flares and some mortar firing, then it just stopped." He took the cup of tea his mother handed to him. "No one seems to be taking much notice of it. The traffic in the town looks quite normal. It may have been manoeuvres."

"That's what they'll probably tell us," she said. "I don't believe it. I think it was another coup."

"It was a flop then," he said. "It's all over."

He gave her a brief smile and touched her shoulder lightly, drank his tea standing, then went indoors, saying that he was going to shave. Mr. Forrest also went indoors to get dressed.

Helena found Mrs. Forrest watching her.

"It looks as if Hugh was right and I shouldn't have woken you," she said. "I'm sorry. It must have been a rather alarming beginning to your stay. But at least Jean doesn't know about it. I don't think she need, do you?"

"I'm sure she needn't," Helena said.

"If it really is all over."

"Don't you think it is?"

"Oh, I'm sure it is. Oh yes, of course." It was a little too hurried. "If Paul thinks so. . . ." Mrs. Forrest picked up the tray and went out with it to the kitchen.

They all met again about half an hour later at breakfast. There was pau-pau with wedges of fresh lime, bacon and eggs and coffee. Because Jean was there, not a word was said about the dawn battle, or whatever it had been. The soft-footed servants came and went without any signs of excitement. Paul ate his breakfast quickly, then disappeared again in the car. He said he was going to see the doctor who was taking over his practice, a young Indian, born in Tondolo but trained in London and Calcutta. Mrs. Forrest said that she would be going into the town shortly to do some shopping and asked Jean and Helena if they would like to go with her. Mr. Forrest went out into the garden again to take another look at the stumps of his pergola. In the big sitting-room one of the servants began polishing the wood-block floors by skating up and down them on what looked rather like snowshoes made of sheepskin. Another servant started washing the tiled floor of the verandah.

An odd thing began to happen to Helena. She began to forget the shooting. First it began to feel unreal to her, then for quite long periods she simply did not remember it at all. But she did not think about much else either. She had slipped into a dreamy, passive state in which she was able to take in very little except such things as had an immediate impact on her senses, the sounds and the scents and the colours.

It was partly the heat, she supposed, and perhaps also the altitude, but what was certainly affecting her more strongly than anything else was the sheer differentness of everything. It filled up her consciousness so that there was not much room for thinking. She found herself contemplating some of the clusters of flowers on a potato tree for minutes on end. Each cluster had an extraordinary variety of colours in it, because when a bud first opened it was deep purple, then it changed to lilac, and finally, before it began to fade, became almost pure white, so that the whole tree was smothered in gay Victorian-looking posies.

Then there was the mystery of the sky. Helena had thought that here on the equator it would be an even more blazing blue than on the Mediterranean. But it was as soft and delicate a blue as the skies of Scotland, and there were always great clouds moving slowly across it, clouds that all had that massive, sculptured look that she had noticed when she first landed.

There was also the curious silence of the house. How could a house so full of servants be so silent? Going about their work they were all so quiet that Helena felt as if she were surrounded by soft-footed jungle creatures, who would prefer that she should be unaware of their nearness.

She remembered having read that the African of the cities is still only a generation away from the forests, where life can depend on the ability to tread noiselessly and to avoid the clumsy movements that betray the hunter to his prey; and that he still dislikes sudden, loud, startling noises. But she found the quiet oddly oppressive. She would have felt much more at ease with more chatter and clatter around her.

Presently Mrs. Forrest appeared and she and Jean and Helena were driven into Tondolo in an oldish, stately Daimler by a sprucely uniformed chauffeur called Erasmus. They went first to the market. It was down one of the older streets of the town and consisted of a few rows of stalls heaped with fruit and vegetables and shaded by canopies of rough thatch. Mrs. Forrest haggled across the piled-up aubergines, tomatoes, cape gooseberries and sweet potatoes as if the few cents that she was able to knock off the price of each purchase might save her family from starvation.

It was accepted as a matter of course, even with a touch of apathy, by the dark-skinned women who sat gossiping behind the heaps of produce. There was none of the passion-ate interest in the bargaining that it would have aroused in countries farther north. Some of the women suckled babies while they weighed out the fruit and vegetables and generally they accepted what Mrs. Forrest offered them without much argument.

"You have to bargain, of course," she told Helena. "They expect it. Even so, they rob us."

Jean was carrying her basket for her and it was gradually filling with delectable-looking things at which Jean looked with great suspicion.

"Can you really eat them, Grandmother?" she asked. "You're sure they aren't poison?"

"Good gracious," Mrs. Forrest said, giving her a rather startled look. "Do you suspect me of wanting to poison you?"

"Well, no, but all the same you are *sure* . . . ?"

"As sure as I can be after eating these things all my life," Mrs. Forrest answered. "You see, you're abroad now, Jean. There are different things to eat as well as different things to look at."

"I like what we have to eat at home," Jean said.

"All children are hopelessly conservative about food," Mrs. Forrest observed to Helena. She went on, "Who does the cooking at home, Jean?"

"We all do it," Jean said. "Anyone who's there."

"You mean *you* can cook?" her grandmother asked.

"Yes, I can cook scones and welsh rarebit."

"And is that what you live on when your mother's away?" Mrs. Forrest asked. "Scones and welsh rarebit?"

"No, Daddy can cook everything," Jean said.

"There!" Mrs. Forrest's voice held a note of fierce triumph. "I knew it. Denis has made a complete mess of his life. I ask you, what chance has he ever had of being happy? It's that woman's fault. In my opinion she isn't entirely human. She'd sacrifice anyone to her insane ambitions . . . Well, we can at least feed Jean up properly now." She added two pounds of avocados, at a few cents a pound, to the basket. "Now we'll go to Patel's. There are a few things I want there. We may as well walk. It's just round the corner."

The basket had become rather heavy for Jean to carry, so Helena took it from her. They turned the corner of the street into one of the broad thoroughfares of the town and went into a moderate-sized self-service shop in which

Vim, Bisto and Heinz soups and everything else that can be bought in any grocery in Britain were on the shelves. The abruptness of the change from the old market round the corner made the place feel unreal to Helena, even made her feel unreal to herself. Was she perhaps not there at all? For the moment she almost felt that her real self was still at home in London's slush and bitter wind.

Mrs. Forrest picked a few things off the shelves and paid the young Indian girl at the door.

Going out into the sunshine again, she stated, "Now you'd like some coffee. And Jean would like an ice. We'll go to Pam's Teashop. But we'll put these things in the car first."

She led them back to where Erasmus was waiting with the car, then on to the teashop.

It was over a souvenir shop that sold such things as beads, carved animals and native drums in all shapes and sizes. The coffee was served on a terrace from which you could see a statue of George V, which stood in the gardens in front of the Ministry of Justice, just as stolidly as if he still had a function to perform.

Another woman who had been drinking coffee on the terrace and was just leaving called out a greeting to Mrs. Forrest and said, "Hear the fireworks this morning, Judy? I thought they were starting things up again, but seems it was only manoeuvres."

"Is that what they're saying? Then there's no need to talk about it, is there?" Mrs. Forrest made a slight warning gesture in Jean's direction. "It isn't really very interesting. By the way, this is my granddaughter, Jean."

"Oh? Oh, I see." The woman smiled at Jean. "We've all heard all about you, of course, Jean. How d'you like Tondolo?"

Jean went into one of her silences, looking fixedly at the ice that had just been put down before her, and not replying.

"Shy," the woman said.

"Very," Mrs. Forrest said.

Helena did not think that Jean was shy at all. She merely

did not like to speak if she was not quite clear in her own mind as to what she wanted to say.

As soon as the woman had left, she said, "As if I'd tell her if I didn't like Tondolo. It wouldn't be polite."

"*Don't* you like Tondolo?" Mrs. Forrest asked, again looking startled and this time a little apprehensive as well. "Don't you like us all, Jean?"

It was pressing Jean to commit herself too far. She went silent again, spooning up her ice.

"I hope she likes us. I do so want her to like us," Mrs. Forrest said. "To wait all this time to see her and then . . . But I think she likes us. Anyway, she likes Bongo." Her face cleared again. She was a woman who found it very easy to convince herself that things were as she wanted them to be.

It was nearly lunch-time when they got back to the house on the hillside. Mr. Forrest was working on his pergola, knocking down what remained of the three pillars, while Wilbraham, the gardener, stood and watched him, leaning on a rake and laughing with delight at the destruction.

Following his wife into the house, Mr. Forrest said, "I've decided the only thing is to dig out the foundations and start all over again. I'll get Paul to help me when he comes back this evening."

However, when Paul returned in the evening, he brought some friends with him and the pergola was left to itself. Mr. and Mrs. Forrest and Helena were sitting on the verandah when the party arrived, while Jean, lying on her stomach on the sofa in the sitting-room, was reading a book about the fauna of Uyowa that Mr. Forrest had found for her.

Paul's friends were a Superintendent of Police, a man from the British Council, and a journalist who worked for a Tondolo newspaper. The journalist's name was Jim Passfield. He was a short, thickset man, with a bull-neck and hair that had already turned grey although he could not have been more than thirty-five. He had a round, dimpled, spectacled face with the mocking blue eyes and sad twisted smile of a lively, intelligent clown. Vernon Elder, the man from the British Council, was tall and slender, with a crumpled-looking, old-young face and earnest eyes. Superintendent Meldrum was an unusually tall man with a heavy build, the kind of fair skin that turns ruddy but never brown, and light reddish hair that was beginning to recede from his freckled forehead.

Over the drinks that appeared, Mr. Forrest explained to Helena that although the local police force was composed mainly of Africans, there were still two or three white officers left, acting in an advisory capacity.

The superintendent claimed to have no information about what had really happened at the barracks that morning.

Giving him a long, ironic look, Mrs. Forrest said, "Oh, come on, Robbie, you're among friends."

He grinned, passing a big hand over the thinning hair on top of his head. "No, really, Judy. It's purely an army matter and nothing to do with the police."

"Manoeuvres," she said. "That's what everyone's saying." He nodded.

"Manoeuvres!" She laughed. "As if anyone believes it."

"I know no reason not to believe it," he said.

"And if you did, you'd keep it to yourself. Point taken, Robbie dear," she said. "I'm sorry if I've been indiscreet. But it would be so nice if someone here would occasionally speak the truth. I believe myself it was an attempted coup to put Kaggwa back in power that somehow went wrong."

"That's what I heard it was," Jim Passfield said. He had a soft, plummy way of speaking, like that of an actor who has trained himself to use an accent which he thinks more socially impressive than the one that comes naturally to him. There was a sardonic note in it, however, that made its artificiality seem only a part of his clownishness. "Of course, they only feed the paper with what they want us to publish, but I heard they made fifteen arrests and obtained a number of confessions. Fifteen confessions, naturally, if there were fifteen arrests."

He smiled as he spoke, but something chilly seemed suddenly to permeate the warm evening air.

Vernon Elder gave a slightly uneasy laugh and said, "That's taking a rather grim view of the situation, Jim. Till we can get more reliable information, I think we might settle for manoeuvres. Anyway, for Kaggwa's sake, I hope it's the truth."

"Well, I personally simply can't believe it," Jim Passfield said. "Somebody's been up to something, but didn't do too well, unlucky fellow."

Mrs. Forrest fixed her full, dark stare on the superintendent's face. "Robbie, is Kaggwa alive?"

He answered patiently, "You probably know as much as I do, Judy. He's thought to be alive."

"Even after this morning?"

Her husband reached for Robbie Meldrum's glass to refill it. "Leave the poor man alone, Judy. You've no right to plague him."

"Speaking for myself," Jim Passfield said, "I believe every rumour I hear in this country. But even if one does that, one never quite keeps up with the things that happen. What I've heard this time, as I was saying, is that there were these fifteen arrests. But I didn't hear that Kaggwa was one of them."

"I suppose you wouldn't consider disclosing the source of your information, Jim," Vernon Elder said. "You're always so much better informed than the rest of us."

"A journalist does not disclose his sources," Jim Passfield answered. "Usually. On this occasion, however, I am sure I may. It was Paul."

"Paul?" His mother turned to him swiftly. "You don't actually know anything, do you, Paul? Or . . ." She paused and seemed to consider. "Do you?"

"I've heard rumours, like Jim." Paul had his usual air of keeping himself noncommittally aloof from the discussion, of merely listening and looking on.

"From patients, or more reliable sources?"

"From everybody I've talked to," Paul said. "And as Jim said, the popular view is that there was an attempted coup this morning, which failed, and which has been followed by a number of arrests—just how many varies. But if there've been arrests, I agree with Jim, you can be pretty sure there've been confessions by now, and perhaps executions."

There was another short, chilling silence. Then Jim Passfield stood up.

"I ought to be going or I'll be in trouble with Peg," he said. "Thanks for the drink, Mrs. Forrest. Perhaps you'll all come over to us one evening soon. I'll get Peg to ring you up and fix something. You haven't been over for a long time."

He went down the verandah steps to his car. A short while afterwards Robbie Meldrum and Vernon Elder followed him.

When they had gone Mrs. Forrest gave a little weary sigh and slumped slightly in her chair. Suddenly she looked tired and old.

"Jean," she called out, "what are you doing?"

"Reading," Jean replied from the sitting-room.

"You read too much," Mrs. Forrest said. "I think you ought to have your bath and go to bed."

"All right," Jean said in her usual obliging way and stood up to go. "Good night, Grandmother. Good night, Grandfather." To the evening air she added tenderly, "And good night, Bongo." As she went upstairs she was still clutching her book.

"What a child!" Mrs. Forrest said when she was out of hearing. "She makes me want to cry, she's so unchildish. Her life so far must have been perfectly terrible. If I have my way . . . No, there's no need to jump on me!" she snapped at Paul, who was about to speak. "I know I can't have my own way all the time. For instance, I couldn't make Robbie Meldrum tell us what he obviously knows. Robbie's one of the men one can't influence, even for his own good. I remember trying to warn him off that dreary woman he married. It was on the rebound, of course, after Cleo refused him." She turned to Helena. "He's another of the men who was quite madly in love with Cleo, and if only she'd married him instead of falling in love with that awful Bulgarian——"

"Czech," her husband said.

"All right, Czech, not that I really know the difference. Well, if she wouldn't have Paul, I wish she'd settled for Robbie."

"It always seems to me that he and Barbara are quite happy together," Mr. Forrest said. "I like Barbara. She's got generosity and commonsense. She and Robbie suit each other very well."

"Oh, you always think other people suit each other," she said. "You never see below the surface. Now I do. I see too much. Take the Passfields, for instance. I can tell you that even if Jim and Peg seem to be happy together, it hasn't been at all good for him. How could it have been, being married to a vulgar little baggage like that, who only married him because he would give her the sort of life out here she could never have had in England? Haven't you noticed how abominably rude she is to her servants? Not that I believe in coddling them, as you know. They don't respect you if you do. But she treats them like animals. And in England she couldn't possibly have afforded to have any at all, in spite of those stories she used to tell when she first came out here about her rich and well-connected family. I've sometimes wondered if Jim actually believed them. He's oddly naïve really, in spite of his knowing air." She stood up. "I'll go up and make sure that Jean doesn't go on reading that book all night."

As she went in both her husband and her son started laughing.

"Dear Judy," Mr. Forrest murmured. "How she would love to rearrange everyone else's lives for them. But she really shouldn't have tried to make poor Robbie talk indiscreetly. It was very wrong of her. And she knew it, of course. She always does. She has almost no conscience."

Chuckling, he got up too and went into the house after her.

It had grown dark in the garden. The lights on the verandah lit up a few yards of lawn and a plumbago, the delicate blue of which they had turned to an almost pure white. There was a scent of gardenias in the air. Helena yawned and remembered that they had all got up very early that morning. But she was having one of her lapses of memory about the incident at dawn. She was finding it very difficult to believe that they had all really sat there, drinking tea and listening to the sound of firing in the distance. She began to feel sure that the firing must, in fact, have been manoeuvres, and that that, probably, was what everyone else actually believed, only they were keeping up their doubts because in this quiet, languorous place it was pleasant to have a little drama to talk about.

She and Paul were silent for some minutes. Then a dark figure with a rifle slouched past in the shadows, saying, "Good evening, *bwana*."

Paul replied, "Good evening, Malcolm."

The night-watchman disappeared into the darkness.

Paul stood up and looked questioningly at Helena to see if she wanted another drink. When she shook her head, he refilled his own glass, went back to his chair and sat down. Nursing the glass in both hands, he stared frowningly into it. When he spoke it was hesitantly, with a kind of reluctance. There was no roughness in his tone. Yet Helena was instantly aware of the hostility that she had felt at their first meeting.

"You know, looking at you," he said quietly, evenly, almost indifferently, "it beats me how you ever got mixed up in this damned affair of Denis's. After all, can you go any lower than helping a man to steal a child from her mother?"

CHAPTER IV

If he had accused Helena of having come to Uyowa with a bomb in her suitcase to assassinate Harvey Mukusa, she could hardly have been more astonished. Momentarily she could not speak.

"If I'm wrong about it, I'm sorry," Paul said.

"Oh," she said, "how nice of you! How very nice! Thank you!"

"Am I wrong?" he asked.

"*Wrong?*" she cried.

"Please," he said, "listen a moment. I'm bad at putting things——"

"But you aren't. No one could have put it more succinctly." She was pleased with that word, succinctly. Her vocabulary always improved when she was in a raging temper. It was probably the result of having well-educated parents. She had never had to fall back on obscenity or profanity to express herself. Long, rather literary words, which she hardly knew that she knew, always came pouring out instead. "And why did I do this lowest of all low things?"

"I seem to have put things a good deal too succinctly," he remarked dryly. "But that precise question has been on my mind ever since I met you yesterday. You weren't at all what I was expecting. I assumed, you see, that you knew what you were doing."

"But I'm not doing it. Nobody's doing it. It's not being done. I've only brought Jean here for a three months' visit."

"Is that what Denis told you?"

"Yes, of course."

"And Marcia?"

"I didn't see her. She was working in Nottingham."

"Did she write to you or telephone?"

"No."

"Then you couldn't say, of your own knowledge, that

51

she knew anything whatever about Jean being sent out of
the country."

Until that moment it had not once occurred to Helena that
this in fact was the truth. She began to feel an uncomfortable
sensation in her stomach.

"No," she admitted. "All the same . . . No, I don't
believe it. I don't believe your brother would do a thing
like that. As a matter of fact, he told me very expressly
that part of my job was to bring Jean home again. And—
and even if he had some sort of idea . . . I don't believe it,
but suppose he did, why should he want to involve me?
Can you explain that? A perfect stranger, who could easily
wreck his plans for him."

"You *are* a perfect stranger, I suppose? Because we've all
been assuming, you know, that you weren't."

It did not penetrate at once. She began to say that of course
she was, that until less than a month ago she had never
even heard of Denis Forrest. Then, like a slap in the face,
his meaning hit her.

He must have seen it happen, for he gave a sardonic little
laugh. "Do you mean to say you haven't realised that
we've all been thinking that you and Denis will be getting
married after the divorce that's almost certainly coming?"

"Divorce?" She gave him a blank look, then pushed
her glass forward. "Give me that drink, please. I think
I'm being stupid."

He picked up the bottle and poured.

"Is there going to be a divorce?" she went on.

"It's our pious hope."

"And that's all it is, isn't it? You yourself only half-
believe what you've just suggested."

"That's true. Just about half. But half a belief can be
very unsettling."

"And, as you said, you're already an unsettled person."
She was glad of the warmth of the whisky in her throat.
"I can think of some rather less kind words for your state
of mind, Paul."

"Don't worry, I've thought of them all myself," he said.

"Well, why don't you simply send a cable to Marcia and

find out the facts? That seems a fairly simple thing to do."

"I'd thought of it," he said, "but I don't happen to know her address in Nottingham, or the name of the theatre where she's working. And if I send a cable to their home in London, it'll go through Denis's hands. Do you know the Nottingham address?"

"No."

"And might not give it to me, even if you did."

"Look," she said furiously, "what do you think of me? That I'm your brother's mistress, and I'm going to be the co-respondent when his wife divorces him, and I've brought Jean out here to prevent her mother getting custody of her, which she'd be certain to do otherwise—you really think all that?"

He got up and sat down again on the low wall that edged the verandah, giving Helena a long, probing look which made her think that as a doctor he was probably very clever at diagnosis, but might not be to be depended on in treatment for tact or patience.

"If I were sure I'm right, I'd take Jean back with me to England next week," he stated.

"She seems very happy here," said Helena.

"That isn't the point. And it isn't that I'm on Marcia's side about the divorce either. It's that I find something too unspeakable about trying to force the issue by abducting Jean."

"Of course I'd agree with you if I thought it had happened," Helena said. "Only you won't believe that, will you? So there doesn't seem to be much point in continuing this discussion."

"Tell me," he said, "do you know about Denis applying for a job at Biriki?"

"I think Cleo said something about it. And your mother said yesterday how much she wished he would, but that's all."

"Yes, well, there happens to be a readership in Economic History going there at the moment, quite a good job in its way. The man who had it before had to retire early because he'd had a couple of heart-attacks, and they've had difficulty finding someone to fill the job. They always find it difficult to get senior men here nowadays, because they won't give long-term contracts. It's understandable. They don't want to find themselves saddled with a new class of white bosses. But they haven't enough fully qualified people themselves yet to fill all the jobs, so they still want people from Britain. But the only sort of people who'll come out on their terms are the old, who've retired already, but think they'd like a salary for another few years to help out with the pension, or else the very young, who want to see the world a bit before they settle down. The people they need here, the people established in their professions, with good reputations, who could help build Biriki into something significant, are the very ones who won't come. Why should they? Why should they throw away a secure future for the sake of God knows what? So someone like Denis could walk straight into that job here. And, as it happens, he wrote to my parents and said he was thinking of sending in an application."

In the warm night Helena felt a coldness sting her nerves. For the first time she wondered seriously if she had been used by Denis Forrest to abduct his daughter.

Paul Forrest was still watching her with that clinically observant gaze.

"Perhaps I should add," he said, "that Marcia wrote immediately afterwards, contradicting it. She added that if he did come, she'd divorce him and that she'd grounds that would make it easy. I didn't take much notice of it at the time. Marcia always hurls threats of divorce around when she gets nervous. She and Denis have always quarrelled a great deal and it's never seemed to mean much. But then I heard you were coming out here with Jean, and letting Jean or Denis get near my mother, who, you may have noticed, is a somewhat possessive person, is something that Marcia's always seemed ready to fight to the death. So we thought that Denis had at last taken things into his own hands——"

"I can tell you something," Helena interrupted in a shrill,

strained voice, "if there's a word of truth in all of this, I'll take Jean home myself immediately. *If* any of it is true. But I don't believe it is. I know some of it isn't. I've met your brother exactly three times, and twice Jean was there— once when we went to the zoo together and once when he saw us off at Victoria. So becoming lovers would have been quick work, wouldn't it?"

She jumped up from her chair, conscious of a dismayed look of uncertainty on Paul Forrest's face, but without waiting for him to answer, she went quickly into the house.

She almost made up her mind that evening to tell the Forrests next day that she must return to England immediately; that it was evident to her that their kind welcome had been obtained on false pretences; that she was not about to become their daughter-in-law, supplanting the detested Marcia. By the morning, however, she had calmed down. Let the Forrests, and particularly Paul, think what they liked, she thought. She had promised Denis Forrest to bring his daughter home in three months' time, and that was what she would do.

Nevertheless, she was glad that next day she hardly saw Paul at all. He was still seeing a few of his patients, and he had left the house before she came down to breakfast. He did not come home for lunch and although he returned for dinner, he went out again immediately afterwards.

That was the day that Wilbraham, the gardener, failed to come to work. Mr. Forrest discovered it when he was taking his usual turn round the garden after breakfast. Coming back into the house, he remarked to his wife, "Wilbraham isn't here, Judy. I do hope that doesn't mean he's left us. He's the best gardener we've had for years."

"Oh, he'll turn up later," Mrs. Forrest said. "He's probably sleeping it off after getting drunk last night."

But Wilbraham did not turn up all day, or the next day either.

"Very tiresome of him," Mr. Forrest said that evening at dinner and explained to Helena, "I expect he's gone into the country to visit his family. That's a way they have. Unfortunately they don't warn you they're going, though you'd be perfectly willing to give them the time off if they'd just ask. They simply take off and then one day they're back again as if nothing has happened. One has to get used to it."

"But doesn't a man like Wilbraham have his family living with him in Tondolo?" Helena asked.

"Oh no, they live a long way away in the country," he said, "where they can just about scrape an existence out of the ground, living almost as they've lived since the beginning of time."

"And don't make any mistake," Mrs. Forrest said, "that's how they want to go on living."

"No, Judy," he disagreed with her. "They want all the things that everyone wants—food, transistors, bicycles, medicines, education—particularly education. I've reason to know that, handling some of the boys I have, brilliant boys like Kaggwa, who came to me straight from one of those villages in the bush. And the only reason a man like Wilbraham works in Tondolo is so that he can make a little extra money here to take back to them there. They've very strong family feelings."

"All the same," Mrs. Forrest said, "you know that if people like us were all to leave—the white people who've stayed on to work here, and the Indians too—the Africans would soon slip straight back into that neolithic sort of life."

"Then why not let them?" Paul asked abruptly. He had done a long day's work and sounded nervous and tired. He seemed particularly edgy too when Helena was about and when he could, he avoided looking at her. "If that's really what they want, why not let them slip back as far as they like, then re-emerge in their own time, in their own way? It's the only way that'll ever be genuine."

"But the waste!" Mrs. Forrest exclaimed. "The waste of everything we've done for them! People like your father—and you too—what you might do, at least, if only you hadn't got this absurd bug in your head about going back to England. Everything would be wasted. Everything."

"I'm not sure that that wouldn't be a lot better than having hundreds of centuries of other people's civilisation jammed down your throats all in seventy or eighty years," Paul said. "But actually what you're afraid of is that if we cleared right out, the Russians or the Chinese would move in. And that wouldn't be very comfortable for you, would it?"

She gave him a long grave look. "I wish I could understand what's happened to you recently, Paul. You quarrel with everything I say. And you used to be such a good-tempered, happy sort of boy. We never had any trouble with you. Just the opposite of Denis. Sometimes when he was a child I thought he'd drive me mad with his tantrums and his illnesses, which Dr. MacKenzie always said were half hysterical. And look how easy he is to get along with now."

There was an appeal in her voice, a need to be assured of Paul's affection.

He did not respond to it, but as if it were the last straw after his exhausting day, got up and left the table.

She sighed and said, "He's in love, that must be what it is. And I do so hope it's Cleo. She and I really understand each other. We've always got on so well. I trust her. If he marries her, I shan't lose him."

"Well, meanwhile I think we ought to be thinking about Jean," Mr. Forrest said. "We ought to be making arrangements to take her to one of the Game Parks. The child's eating her heart out because she hasn't seen an elephant yet."

Mrs. Forrest nodded but frowned slightly. "I know. We'll have to do something about it. She's getting almost melancholic. Very like Denis, as a matter of fact, when he couldn't have what he wanted. But the thought of driving right out into the bush just at the moment rather worries me."

He looked surprised. "Why?"

"Because we still don't know what that shooting the other morning was all about."

"Oh, that. I don't think we need worry about it. Everything seems to be functioning perfectly normally."

"But I heard from Vernon Elder when I met him in

town this morning that there's supposed to be a State of Emergency in the country and that he got stopped by soldiers who stuck a rifle in at the window of his car when he was only driving over to Igambo to see some friends off on the plane to Nairobi."

"There's been a so-called State of Emergency ever since Mukasa took over," Mr. Forrest said, "but I haven't heard of any interruption in the tourist traffic to the Game Parks. I think we might arrange something for this week-end. I believe we'd have to get permits to travel, but that's all."

"Please, Hugh!" Mrs. Forrest put her fists on the table. There was extreme tension in her voice. "Please! Be serious for a moment. Don't go on keeping up this pretence there's nothing wrong. We're responsible for Jean, aren't we?"

"Of course."

"If anything should happen . . ."

"Nothing will."

"But if it did!"

He gave a rather sad shake of his head. "All right. But you're fussing too much, you know, my dear. It isn't good for children to feel you're worrying over them too much."

"Didn't I bring up my own two sons perfectly successfully?" she demanded.

"I'm afraid that's the kind of question to which there's no answer, since the standard of success has not been settled," he said. "You don't seem particularly satisfied with Paul at the moment. However, if you feel so strongly about it . . . I think you're wrong though."

Helena also thought that Mrs. Forrest might be wrong. Jean had been very listless all that day. She had played with Bongo in the garden, had gone shopping in the town with Mrs. Forrest, had gone a walk with Helena along the shady roads of the suburb on the hillside, and had lain on her stomach on the sofa, reading. But there were no other children for her to play with and Helena believed that she was more homesick than she wanted anyone to know. She needed distraction.

But Helena did not express her opinion. Ever since her talk with Paul, she had become self-conscious and tongue-tied with the Forrests, suspicious of their kindness to her. At times she wanted to tell them openly that she was not an accomplice in the abduction of their grandchild. At other times she thought that no one but Paul had ever imagined that she was.

Next day Jean asked Helena when she thought that they would visit a Game Park. They were in Pam's Teashop. They had been driven into the town by Erasmus, because Helena wanted to cash a travellers' cheque, and for once they were without Mrs. Forrest, who had been invited to a coffee-party by a Mrs. Chokwe, the wife of a High Court judge.

Helena and Jean had gone into the first bank that they had come to, finding long queues at every cashier's window of people who looked as if they expected to stand there for hours, perhaps all day, and who would not mind it much if they had to. They had been quiet, with the curious quiet that Helena had noticed among the servants in the Forrests' house. There had been no pushing or shoving or chattering, just a relaxed and patient stillness. Luckily there had been no queue at the desk where travellers' cheques were cashed and Helena and Jean had emerged fairly quickly, then had set off for the teashop, and on the way had happened to pass a tourist agency, where Jean had stopped. She had pressed her nose to the window, had stared for a long time at a poster showing an elephant family, two big elephants with a little one between them, which advertised bus trips to the Ross Falls National Game Reserve, then she had sighed deeply. As she and Helena had gone on Jean had remained silent, evidently thinking hard. It was when they were on the terrace of the teashop that she spoke suddenly.

"Helena, are you very busy?"

"No, not at all," Helena answered. "Not in the very least."

"Then do you think you and I could do something together?"

"I'm sure we could," Helena said. "What are you thinking of?"

"If we could go to that place . . . Ross Falls."

"Oh—oh, I see."

Jean was watching Helena's face very intently for her reaction. "Wouldn't you like to go?"

"Yes, of course, Jean, but I—I think we'll all be going together sometime soon in any case," Helena said. "Anyway, I hope so."

"But it's soon now!" Jean said violently. "We've been here *days*."

"Oh, only a few days."

But a few days can be a very long time to an impatient child.

"I don't think we're going at all!" Jean said in a low voice of startling passion. "Daddy promised we'd go, but nothing's happening."

"Are you very bored then?" Helena asked.

"Oh, I'm not *bored*—I'm just worried in case we really aren't going ever. But Daddy *promised*."

"I'm sure we'll go sooner or later," Helena said. "I expect your grandparents are too busy at the moment."

"But couldn't you and I go by ourselves?" Jean said. "Or is it very expensive? You aren't rich like Grandmother, are you?"

Helena laughed. "No, I'm not. And I didn't actually notice how much the trip costs."

"It costs three hundred shillings," Jean said. "Is that a lot?"

"Well, the Uyowan shilling is worth just about the same as our shilling, so three hundred is fifteen pounds."

"Oh, that *is* a lot, isn't it?" Jean's face fell. "I haven't got that much money in all the world. I don't suppose you could afford it, could you?"

"Perhaps I could. Anyway, I'll see what I can do. I'll talk to your grandparents about it. Perhaps, if they're too busy, they'll let you and me go off together."

"After all, we came here together, didn't we?" Jean said. "And that's much farther than Ross Falls and cost much more."

"That's true. Well, I'll see what I can do. I really will, Jean."

"To-day?"

"To-day."

Not that it would be much use, Helena thought, remembering the argument between Mr. and Mrs. Forrest on the subject.

However, she intended to keep her promise and made up her mind to approach Mr. Forrest on Jean's behalf later that day. But, as it happened, she had no opportunity of doing so. He went out in the afternoon and, in the evening, when Jean had been put to bed, the Forrests took Helena to the Passfields' house for drinks, where there were far too many people for there to be any possibility of bringing the matter up.

The Passfields lived in a house on the hillside on the far side of the town, a house very like the Forrests', except that it was smaller and had an uncared-for look, as if perhaps there were not really enough money to keep it up. Yet there seemed to be as many servants to carry round the drinks as at the Forrests'.

The talk was mostly about people whom Helena did not know, and there was a certain amount of talk about the firing in the morning three days ago. Superintendent Meldrum, who was there with his pleasant-looking wife, Barbara, was still as evasive about it as he had been on the day it happened. Mrs. Passfield laughed at him for it. She was a small-boned, pallid woman, restless and ineffectual, who tried to make up for her colourlessness by incessant talk.

"Of course he knows all about it, but you don't think he'd tell us a single thing, do you?" she said in a thin, strident voice that carried all over the room. "Jim's the same. He always says that what I don't know I can't pass on. That's a man for you. He knows I'm not a gossip. I can't bear gossip. It's all so dull. Yet that's all anyone ever does here—talk, talk, talk, and all about one another. It's so boring, it makes me go screaming mad. It isn't as if people ever say interesting things about each other. They haven't any interests to talk about."

"Then why don't you go home, my dear," Mrs. Forrest asked, "if you think you'd find people more interesting there?"

"Home!" Mrs. Passfield said scornfully. "Go back to that climate? And all the restrictions, the taxes—God, what a thought! You know what, the whole world's becoming an impossible place to live in. If it isn't one thing, it's another."

"Robbie, that reminds me," Mr. Forrest said, "do we still need permits to travel?"

"Yes, as a matter of fact, you do," Robbie Meldrum answered. "Not that there's any difficulty about getting them. Why?"

"We're thinking of taking Jean and Helena to one of the Game Parks."

"We are not!" Mrs. Forrest said swiftly. "Not yet. Not if Robbie won't tell us what that shooting was about. We're responsible for Jean and I'm not taking any risks till I know what the situation is. I don't believe for a moment in that story of manoeuvres. I believe it was an attempted coup by Kaggwa's friends and that there'll be another one. And I only hope they do better next time. Gilbert Kaggwa is an intelligent, liberal-minded man whom I very much admire. As I expect I've said before, he was one of Hugh's best pupils and he was a friend of Denis's at Oxford. . . . Oh, thank you," she added absently, taking a sausage on a stick from a plate offered to her by a dark-faced servant. "Yes, as I was saying, I only hope Kaggwa's still alive and that next time they make a good job of it."

"And I only hope our boy didn't understand what you were saying, Mrs. Forrest," Jim Passfield said in his soft, plummy, actor's voice. He had just joined the group. "I don't trust any of them myself. I think almost everything we say gets reported to certain quarters."

Mrs. Passfield gave a crow of laughter. She threw a thin arm round his neck. "Darling, the brute can't even speak English, only that awful pidgin. He's an absolute clot. They're all absolute clots. They make me go screaming mad. They don't know the first thing. And if you don't keep after them all the time, they just sit down and go to sleep . . ." She was launched on a tirade against her servants.

Mrs. Forrest endured it, tight-lipped, for a few minutes, then caught her husband's eye, made the faintest of grimaces and as soon as possible they left.

Robbie Meldrum went with them to their car. His ruddy face was serious.

"Hugh, there's something I want to tell you, though I'm not sure if I should," he said, uneasily smoothing back the thin hair from his freckled forehead. "It's only a rumour, but in case you've been worried—the story is that that gardener of yours, Wilbraham Ngugi, is being held for questioning in connection with an attempt on the life of Mukasa. I—I honestly don't know if it's true or not. The police aren't always told these things, whatever Judy thinks."

"Good God—Wilbraham?" Mr. Forrest exclaimed. "Poor devil."

"But that does mean it was an attempted coup the other morning!" Mrs. Forrest cried.

Robbie Meldrum shook his head. "Not necessarily. This attempt on Mukasa's life was a couple of days earlier than the shooting. A grenade was thrown at his car when he was on his way home from a reception at the Institute of Technology. They've been keeping it very quiet. But I thought I'd tell you about it in case they come and question you about Ngugi. And I think it's possible—just possible, Judy—that Passfield was right when he hinted you shouldn't go in for too much reckless talk just at the moment. Things are a bit touchy." He smiled. "Not that I've ever known anyone who could stop Judy saying what came into her head. Good night."

He returned to the party.

No one spoke much on the way home. The superintendent's words seemed to have had some effect on Mrs. Forrest. She sat smoking a cigarette and frowning. The streets of the town were silent and deserted. If there had not been a few people strolling along the almost empty pavements, it would have been easy to imagine that there was a curfew in force. The busy crowds of the daytime had all vanished into the darkness. What Helena had begun to think of as the African silence had the town in its grip.

When the Forrests reached home, dinner was waiting for them. But first Mrs. Forrest went upstairs to take a look at Jean.

"Fast asleep," she said when she came down again. "She's settling down very well, isn't she?"

It was a moment when Helena might have said that the truth about Jean was that she was not settling down at all well, and was not actually very happy. But after hearing what Superintendent Meldrum had said, Helena was more impressed than she had been before by the possible risk to the child of taking her, just then, to one of the Game Parks.

Most of the white people here, she was beginning to realise, were not, as she had thought at first, over-dramatising the dangers of their lives, but actually were in a state of far greater tension than they wanted to admit. In spite of the sunny comfort of their existences, there were thoughts at the backs of all their minds of the Congo and Nigeria. So she stuck to her plan of waiting until she had an opportunity to discuss Jean's problems, perhaps after dinner, with Mr. Forrest.

But after dinner Paul and his mother had a quarrel. Helena did not know what it was about; she only heard raised voices in the dining-room after she and Mr. Forrest had gone out to the verandah for coffee. Then Paul slammed out of the room and went upstairs to his room. A moment later Mrs. Forrest came out on to the verandah, breathing quickly, and with harsh patches of red on her cheeks.

Mr. Forrest poured out a cup of coffee and put it down beside her.

"You shouldn't try to stop him going now, you know, Judy," he said. "It's too late. And I'm sure he's doing what's best for someone of his generation."

She pressed her lips together, looking as if she did not mean to answer. But then she burst out; "He shouldn't go,

he shouldn't. If we could be sure that Denis was coming . . .
But suppose he doesn't."

"Then we'll just have to get on without them," Mr.
Forrest replied. "You and I. It was bound to come to
that sooner or later, anyway."

"Helena, is Denis coming?" Mrs. Forrest demanded,
turning on her sudenly. "You should know."

Caught unawares, Helena stammered, "I? I don't know
anything, Mrs. Forrest."

"Don't you. Don't you truly?"

"No."

Mrs. Forrest glowered darkly at her. "We've all thought
he was coming."

"I'm sorry. I really don't know anything about it."

Mrs. Forrest turned abruptly away. "If only I'd had a
daughter," she muttered fiercely.

"She'd have gone too," Mr. Forrest said. "Daughters
aren't what they were."

"But you don't lose a daughter as completely as a son,"
she said. "She wants you to help her when she has her
children. She wants you at all sorts of times. Cleo's the
nearest I've ever had to a daughter, d'you know that? If
only she'd married Paul, Hugh!"

"Well, perhaps she'll marry him now, if you're right that
that's why he's going home."

"Home—you always say home. This is home."

"Yes, yes, of course, it's just that the word slips out."

"You wouldn't care for it yourself if you went back, you
know . . ."

Helena felt that they had both forgotten that she was
there on the verandah with them. Getting up quietly, she
murmured good night and went up to her room.

It was early to go to sleep, so she read for a time before
turning out the light, but when she did she slept almost
at once and heavily. When she woke it was still dark.
Rubbing her eyes, she peered round the room in confusion,
because she had a muddled, dreamy certainty that she had
heard her door being softly closed. But the feeling passed.

C

Turning her head on the pillow, she saw through the window the flame-colour of the dawn and heard a few birds begin to sing, then in a moment she was asleep again.

She woke later when one of the servants came in with her morning tea. She was still in a drowsy stupor as she poured it out. Then all of a sudden she was wide awake. Jumping out of bed, she ran across the road to her dressing-table, where, propped against the looking-glass, there was a sheet of paper. On it, in large, careful letters, was written: "Dear Helena, I am sorry about the money, but Grandmother wil give it to you as she has lots, I nede three hundred shillings, you said, so that is what I took, I am going to look at the elefants, I will be back soon, Your loving Jean."

Beside the note lay Helena's handbag, open.

She wasted time reading the note twice. She even looked in her handbag. Most of the money that she had cashed the day before was gone. Snatching up her dressing-gown, she ran out into the passage and into Jean's room. It was empty. It was also very tidy. The bed had been made. There were no clothes lying about. It looked almost as if Jean had not slept there, but at some time in the night, all alone, aged seven, with fifteen pounds' worth of Uyowan shillings to support her, had set off into the African bush.

CHAPTER V

"We must not lose our heads," Mr. Forrest said. "We must not panic."

No one was showing any sign of panic, unless it were the stony silence in which Mrs. Forrest sat, staring at the paper that Helena had thrust into her hand.

Helena and the three Forrests had gathered once more in their dressing-gowns on the verandah, but this time all the servants stood in a close group in the sitting-room, anxiously listening. Helena could tell them apart now. There was Malcolm, the night-watchman. There was Erasmus, the chauffeur. There was Horace, the cook, a mercurial, smiling man, who giggled cheerfully in answer to almost anything that was said to him. There was Josiah, a houseboy, ageing and grizzled, who had been with the Forrests for years, and whose face always wore a remote look as of someone listening to something in the distance. The other house-boy, Joe, was a very good servant, efficient and punctual, but temperamental, with dark moods of animosity to his employers and his fellow servants.

They had all been questioned by Mr. Forrest and all had denied having seen Jean leave the house.

Paul gestured at the letter. "That's genuine, I suppose?"

His mother answered, "Of course it's genuine. I've been a fool. I know enough about children, I ought to have seen what was going on in her. She was unhappy with us and I ought to have done something about it."

There was deep anger in her tone. Yet it did not sound as if the anger were directed against herself so much as against the fates for having forced her into the false position of being wrong.

"I meant, I suppose she did write it herself, she did go off of her own free will," Paul said.

They all looked at him.

Mr. Forrest said softly, "Oh God!"

"I ought to tell you," Helena said quickly, "she's done it before. Denis warned me. He told me she once set off to look for the North Pole. And once they had to get the police to look for her and they found her riding round and round on the Underground. And she's always going off alone to feed the pigeons in Trafalgar Square. I ought to have remembered it."

"It's not your fault," Paul said. "You couldn't keep a twenty-four hour watch on her."

Still in an angrily bitter tone, Mrs. Forrest said, "She was there when I went in to look at her after we got back from the party. She was sound asleep. Everything looked normal. How could I guess . . . ?"

"We're wasting time," Paul said. Of the three Forrests, he looked the most like himself, the least affected, and so the likeliest to be capable of decisive action. "We may as well assume for the moment that Jean went off by herself, just as she said, to see elephants. Then how did she go about it? She got dressed, helped herself to Helena's money and slipped quietly out of the house when Malcolm was looking the other way. She then walked down into the town. She knows the way, she's been driven in a number of times, and certainly the distance wouldn't be too much for her. She then must have gone to the tourist agency that Helena tells us they looked into yesterday morning, though there are others, of course, that she could have gone to. But questioning Helena as carefully as she did immediately after looking into that particular window, and taking the exact amount of money she knew she'd need to buy a ticket from them, suggests to me that that's where she'd go."

"But nobody there would sell her a ticket," Mrs. Forrest said. "An unaccompanied child of seven. They're responsible people, they'd never do it."

"I don't think they would," Paul replied. "So it seems to me very likely that she's in their office now, kicking her heels in a very bad temper and refusing to tell them who she is or where she comes from. And they've either telephoned the police about her already or are waiting in the hope that someone will turn up to claim her."

"I think we ought to telephone the police now ourselves," Mrs. Forrest said.

"Unless you wait till I've been down to the tourist people," Paul said. "It's quite likely we'll find her there."

"I'll go with you," Helena said.

"All right, if you can get dressed in five minutes." He went upstairs to get dressed himself.

A few minutes later, when Helena came down from her room, wearing slacks, shirt and sandals, Mrs. Forrest was putting the telephone down. There was still the sound of smouldering rage in her voice.

"Not there!" she said. "Robbie Meldrum's not there, just when we need him. He's been sent off to investigate trouble in one of the villages. Something about some suspected ritual murders. Thirteen people killed by witchcraft. I wonder if it's true."

"Why shouldn't it be true?" her husband asked. "These things happen, even if the witchcraft turns out to be some fairly commonplace poison."

"I mean, is it true that Robbie's not there? You know how they love to obstruct one."

"You should have told them what had happened, not just asked for Robbie, then we'd have got all the help we wanted," he said. "But perhaps Paul's right that we ought to wait till he's been round the agencies before we try again."

"We shan't get any help from them, even then," she muttered. "You know how they love to remind one who's got the power now."

"Over a lost child? Here, let me try. . . ."

He was thrusting her away from the telephone as Paul and Helena left the house.

"It isn't true, is it, that the police won't help?" she said as they drove off. "Are they really as bad as that?"

"Of course not," Paul said. "They've some very good men. But sometimes they've more on their hands than they can cope with."

"So your mother might be right."

"My mother," he replied, "is a solid rock of prejudice, under the faint tolerance that's rubbed off on her from my father. In a crisis her real feelings emerge, and though she'd never forgive me for saying so, they're pretty much the same as Peg Passfield's. There may be more feudal dignity in my mother's attitude, yet she doesn't actually think that Africans are human."

"And do you?"

"I? Oh, I'm full of prejudices of all kinds, as you've noticed," he said. "Like Jean, I've a bit of a prejudice against the human race. Look, if you want a serious discussion of the colour problem, couldn't we set some other time for it?"

"I'm sorry," Helena said. "I was talking to keep my mind off Jean. If we don't find her at the tourist agency, what do we do next?"

"Try the other agencies."

"And if we don't find her in any of them?"

"Go home."

"And leave it to the police?"

"What else can we do? Helena. . . ." All the time that they had been talking, she had seen that he had been concentrating on some thought of his own. "You probably know Jean a little better than the rest of us. Is she the kind of child who'd take up with some complete stranger?"

"I shouldn't have thought so," Helena said. "She's not too keen on taking up with anyone at all."

"So if she left the house by herself, as it seems evident she did, she isn't likely to have gone off with someone she'd just picked up, who promised to show her some animals."

"Oh, if he promised to show her animals . . ."

Suddenly she felt more afraid than she had since she had first seen Jean's note. She tried to say that she did not know, but her voice dried up.

Paul gave her a quick glance.

"I really shouldn't worry too much yet," he said. "She's probably safer here than she'd be in a London suburb. I mean it. She'll be more conspicuous and much easier to

trace, and she'll know much less about how to go about
things by herself."

"Yes—yes, I suppose so."

"I should say we're practically certain to find her at that
tourist agency."

But they did not find her there.

With the poster of the happy elephant family that had
so attracted Jean on the wall above her desk, a young Indian
woman in a neat, tailored linen suit listened to them with
attention, shook her head and told them that she was quite
sure that no child had attempted to buy a ticket for any
of the bus tours that morning; that if one had come in by
herself, she would certainly not have been sold a ticket;
that there had, as a matter of fact, been no children on
any of the buses that had already gone off. She called one
or two other clerks in the office over to her desk to corrobor-
ate what she had said, then she took Helena and Paul out
to the car-park from which the buses set out and asked
the attendant there if he had seen a child get on to any
bus or attempt to get on to one.

There was no doubt in his answer that he had not.

"Well, where next?" Helena asked as she and Paul
returned to the car.

"The other companies," he said. "There are two others
and they're quite near here. She may have noticed them."

"But this is surely the one she'd have come to if we're
right about what she's probably done. Don't you think
we've already gone wrong?"

"Perhaps. But we'd better try the other places all the
same."

They said no more until Paul stopped the car outside
the next tourist agency.

They were less helpful here but quite as definite that
no child of seven, accompanied or unaccompanied, had
travelled on any of their buses that morning. As a matter
of fact, the bored clerk who answered their questions told
them, his company ran only one tour that day and he
himself had checked the passengers. There had been no

children among them. He picked his teeth and yawned at them.

The third agency, Happytime Tours Ltd., looked less promising than the other two. It was smaller and shabbier, its posters were dusty and its windows needed cleaning. However, it was here that they at last heard news of Jean. A slim, shirt-sleeved young African who had learnt at least ·some of his English from American films, answered them readily, "Sure, sure, I know the kid you mean. The pretty little kid with the dark hair who came in here with the blonde young lady. Very swell young lady. They went off this morning to Ross Falls. That's a good tour. You like to go too? Too late for to-day, but we run a very good tour there every Tuesday and Friday. See the Falls, the Game Park, spend the night at the Ross Falls Lodge, trip on the river next day, lots of hippopotamus and crocodiles——"

"Please," Paul interrupted, "the child and the young lady. We'll think about going the tour another day, but just now we want to know about the child and the young lady. When did the bus leave for Ross Falls?"

"Eight-thirty," the young man answered. "Punctually. We are always very punctual."

"And you're sure this child was on it? I just want to be certain we're talking about the same one. She's a rather sturdy child with dark hair cut in a sort of ragged way."

"Sure, sure, and a way of looking at you as if she was going to eat you, and wearing blue jeans and kind of a red blouse."

Helena drew a quick breath. "That's right. That's what she had on yesterday."

"Now about the young lady she was with," Paul said. "What was she like?"

"Tall, thin, black glasses, dressed the way they all dress, scarf on her head, trousers, shirt, camera."

"You said she was blonde," Paul said.

"Oh yes. Sure. She was blonde."

"But if she'd a scarf over her hair and dark glasses, how could you tell?"

"Well, maybe she wasn't blonde. Just pale. Very pale. Paler than you or this young lady."

"A newcomer, then. Not been out in the sunshine much. Did she and the child seem to know one another well?"

The clerk gave a wriggle in his swivel chair.

"Look, please!" he said in a high and suddenly excited voice, "I try to tell you everything you want to know, but how do I know a thing like that? You and this young lady come in here, do I know if you are husband and wife? Brother and sister? Do I know what you are? Do I ask? Look, I am a busy man, very busy, I do not conduct examinations of our passengers, I do not make them fill in forms, I do not ask where were you born, who were your father and mother, where were they born, what is your religion? You want to go to Ross Falls, I ask for your names and addresses and three hundred shillings for each and I give you your tickets."

"And what about our travel permits?" Paul asked. "There's supposed to be a State of Emergency in Uyowa. Shouldn't we need travel permits to leave Tondolo? Didn't this woman and child need them?"

The clerk waved his hand. "The company fixes all that. No trouble for the passenger. You want to go next Tuesday, you tell me now, we have the permits before then."

"But suppose we'd come in earlier this morning and wanted to go to-day, could we have bought our tickets and gone straight off or should we have had to wait a day or two for the permits to come through?"

"To-day the bus is full," the young man answered. "Nothing I can do about that. Nothing. Much better always to book in advance."

"What I'm really trying to find out is whether this young lady booked in advance for herself and the child, or appeared for the first time this morning," Paul said.

"Look, please!" The young man's voice rose again into shrillness. "Everyone books in advance! I tell you it is much better! And now I am a busy, busy man. If you do not want to book, I am very busy."

"But can't you tell me when this lady booked?" Paul asked patiently.

"Two days ago," the clerk said.

Paul looked surprised at his positiveness. "Are you sure?"

"Sure, sure, I am sure!"

"In that case, thank you very much for your help."

Paul stood up. The clerk jumped up from his chair too, white teeth flashing in his dark face again in the warmest of smiles.

"Not at all, not at all, a great pleasure. I am very happy to have helped."

He saw Paul and Helena to the door of the office.

Outside, where the heat of the sun, after the dim and dusty office, struck them like a blow in the face, Helena exclaimed, "Two days ago! She bought the tickets two days ago!"

"I don't know," Paul said. "That answer came too quickly and much too exactly, considering he didn't look up any records. He was fed up with us and wanted to get rid of us, so he said the first thing that came into his head. But at least I'd say it was probable, because of the travel permit complication, that the woman, whoever she is, did book two tickets in advance."

"Then was the rest of it true? Is Jean on that bus with her?"

"He got Jean's clothes right, didn't he? And her way of looking at you, if she deigns to look at you at all."

"What do we do now, then?"

"That's simple. Chase the bus." He looked at his watch as they got back into the car. "It left at eight-thirty. It's just on nine-thirty now. We'll catch it up easily."

"Do you know the way to Ross Falls?"

"Oh yes, and the bus will be making a stop for lunch at a place called Lubamba. They always do. So if we don't catch it up before that, we'll get it there."

"What about letting your parents know what we're doing?"

"Oh, we'll go home first," he said. "In the circumstances, they may want to call off the police hunt."

She looked at him curiously. He seemed to have gone very cool and calm all of a sudden.

"I'm afraid I still don't understand what's happened," she said. "This woman none of us know anything about appears out of the blue, buys two bus tickets at least two or three days ago, meets Jean and takes her off to look at Ross Falls. Who in God's name is going to do a thing like that, and what's she done it for?"

"Well, my guess is the woman's simply some fool of a tourist," he said. "Perhaps she bought two tickets because she thought someone else was going with her, and whoever it was let her down. So she went into the office this morning, hoping she could sell the spare ticket back and Jean somehow got hold of her and it. You know what that child's like when she's set her heart on something. And the fifteen pounds may have meant quite a lot to the woman."

"All the same, she'd have to be a more than average fool to go off like that with a strange child," Helena said.

Paul turned out of the main street into the road leading up the hillside. If his manner was cool, there was not much coolness in his driving. He had taken the car through the middle of Tondolo at a speed that had made other drivers turn and swear.

"At least she's a woman, not a man," he said. "Doesn't that allay some of one's more obvious fears? And it doesn't look like a kidnapping. Who's going to kidnap a child by taking her off on a tourist bus? And we know Jean went off this morning of her own free will."

Helena nodded. Yet her mind seethed with doubts and her nerves refused to be set at rest. She thought of that soft closing of her bedroom door that morning, the sense that someone had just been in her room. If only she had taken the trouble to wake up properly then, to get up and investigate, she would have seen Jean's note on her dressing-table, would have caught her before she was out of the house. . . .

"If you're blaming yourse! " Paul broke in on her musing, after giving her one of his brief, perspicacious glances, "you're much less to blame than the rest of us. And Jean probably twisted that silly woman round her little finger with no difficulty at all."

"I wish I really believed that."

"What is it you don't believe?"

"That anyone—anyone at all—could be *so* silly."

He did not answer and Helena suddenly realised that he was far less confident of his own explanation than he had tried to appear.

As he turned the car in at the gate, Mr. Forrest came out to meet them. Mrs. Forrest sat stiff and still on a chair on the verandah, just as if she had not moved all the time that they had been gone.

"Well?" Mr. Forrest asked.

"She's gone off on one of the Happytime buses to Ross Falls," Paul said. "She apparently found some woman she persuaded to take her. What about the police? Are they doing anything?"

"We didn't call them in the end," Mr. Forrest replied. "We thought we'd wait to hear what you discovered. And in the circumstances I'm glad. We want to get the child back with the least fuss possible. That'll be the best thing for her."

"I'll start now then," Paul said. "If I don't catch up with the bus before, I'll do it in Lubamba, when they're at lunch." He went into the house and called into the kitchen. "Josiah, put some beer and sandwiches into the car, will you?"

His mother followed him into the house. "This woman, Paul, what was she like?"

"Tall, thin, dark glasses, scarf over her head, slacks, camera, no tan, probably blonde."

"Marcia!" she cried.

Both Paul and his father stared at her as if she had gone out of her mind.

Mr. Forrest said, "Judy dear, that's one of the most preposterous suggestions I've ever heard."

She pounded the back of a chair with her tight fists. "Of course it's Marcia—tall, thin, blonde! She's realised all along that Denis might be coming to Biriki, that Jean might be staying here, that if she went ahead with her idea of divorcing Denis she might lose Jean altogether too—so she's acted first to get her back."

"And taken her off on a slow bus to a Game Park, instead of straight to the airport?" Paul said mockingly. "You're implying besides that Marcia thought Helena wasn't to be trusted to take Jean home and you've no justification for assuming anything of the kind. I'm going now. Want to come, Helena?"

She was answering that of course she did when Mrs. Forrest interrupted, "Hugh, go with them! You don't lose your head in a crisis."

He looked at her uncertainly. "It doesn't sound as if there's going to be much of a crisis, Judy, and it means leaving you alone."

"You know I don't mind that. And if you don't find Jean at Lubamba you can telephone and I can still get in touch with the police. You'll do that—you'll telephone if you don't find her, won't you?"

Paul said, "I can telephone."

"I don't trust you," she said. "Not any more. I don't understand you any more. You've changed. This idea of leaving us—and contradicting everything I say. Of course this woman's Marcia. Any fool could have guessed that. And of course she doesn't trust Helena. Helena's on our side. It's you who isn't. So I want Hugh to go with you." The violence in her voice dropped. "No, I'm sorry, Paul, I'm sorry, I didn't mean any of it, except that I don't understand you. And Hugh does keep his head, he always knows what to do."

"Well, one thing we might do, I think," Mr. Forrest said, "is take a few overnight things with us. I don't feel at all sure at the moment just where we're going to end up."

He went upstairs. Paul, his face white and furious, followed him.

Helena hesitated for a moment, wanting to tell Mrs. Forrest how wrong she was about her, that she was not on her side but had every intention of honouring her undertak-

ing to Jean's parents. But she sensed that nothing would
get through the older woman's burning preoccupation with
her hatred of her daughter-in-law, on to whom she appeared
to have shifted all the guilt that was gnawing at her because
of what she felt to be her own negligence where Jean was
concerned. So Helena went upstairs too and packed her overnight bag.

As she came downstairs a few minutes later, she found
the puppy Bongo whining uneasily at the signs of prepara-
tions for departure. It was his instinct to try to keep his
human flock all in one place and he already appeared to be
vaguely disturbed by Jean's absence, sniffing about and
barking and growling at nothing. Suddenly he deposited
his hindquarters on Helena's feet to try to prevent her going
any farther. Horace, the cook, saw it and was shaken by
a gale of giggles. It was to the sound of this laughter that
Paul, his father and Helena drove off.

None of them spoke for some time. Paul's face had
kept the white and bitter look that had been brought
to it by Mrs. Forrest's tirade. She'd really lost him now,
Helena thought. He'd go back to England and it might be
years before his mother saw him again. Sitting beside him,
Helena wondered if he had meant it when he said that his
mother had no justification for thinking that Marcia did not
trust Helena. If he had meant it, his own attitude to
herself must have undergone a considerable change during
the last few days. But he might have said it merely to needle
his mother. The two of them were spending their last
few days together in a state of increasing strife.

In the back of the car Mr. Forrest sat with the tips of his
fingers pressed together and a thoughtful look on his face.
It was he who spoke first, as the car, travelling fast, left the
pleasant white houses and shady gardens behind and went
on between scattered banana and tapioca plantations and
high red ant-hills. There were low thatched huts on each side
of the road, around which almost naked children played,
and massive women in splendidly coloured robes strolled
heavily, usually with water-jugs or laden baskets on their
heads.

"I think what worries me most," Mr. Forrest said at last, "is that she'd have to be literally a lunatic to do it—this tall, thin woman in dark glasses. To let a strange child persuade her into taking her on a two-day bus trip. I mean, she'd have to be really mentally sick, like those unfortunate women without children of their own, who mean no evil, but suddenly can't resist the temptation to help themselves to someone else's baby out of its perambulator. And, after all, mental sickness is appallingly common."

"But I suppose it's still a less frightening hypothesis than . . ." Helena boggled at the next word.

"Kidnapping." Paul said. "Yes, as long as we catch up with the bus. If not—well, the insane are unpredictable."

"And I suppose we shall catch up with it," his father said. "The road gets pretty bad soon and those damned buses are built for them, which this car isn't."

"Oh, we'll catch it."

"Suppose the woman leaves the bus at Lubamba."

"We can probably pick up her trail. She'd have to hire a car, for one thing, and I'm not sure that she could do that in a hurry. There's almost nothing there but the hotel."

"Yes. . . . Yes, but there's another thing that's worrying me, Paul. The more I think about it, the more it worries me. It's Josiah. I've known him so long and I think he was lying this morning when he said he hadn't seen Jean leave. It's only a feeling I've got, a sort of uneasiness. But you know that faraway look of his, that sort of look of not being in the same world as you. Well, when he lies he looks at you very directly and attends to you very carefully."

"I know what you mean."

Paul swung the car off the main road on to a road of red murram. At once the going was bumpier and as they passed a lorry jolting slowly along a cloud of red dust came up chokingly into the car. They hurriedly wound the windows up.

"And he was doing that this morning, was he?" Paul asked. "Looking you in the eye and listening."

"I think so. That's how I remember it now, though I was too upset at the time to take it in."

"But even if he did see Jean go and lied about it," Paul said, "it was probably only to avoid trouble. I can't imagine him wanting any harm to come to her."

"No, nor can I. And I noticed that he and she were getting on particularly well. It reminded me of how fond of him you and Denis were as children. But if only I'd thought more clearly at the time, we might have got some information out of him. He may know if she really did walk out and set off into the town all by herself." Mr. Forrest let his hands fall limply between his knees in a gesture of great weariness. He looked fragile and old. "I think so slowly these days and I get confused. A few years ago I'd never have missed a thing like that."

"It probably isn't very significant."

"I hope not, I hope not. And I hope we weren't wrong not to call the police. If only Robbie Meldrum hadn't been away. Judy doesn't really trust any of the others, even the British. She says they aren't real policemen, but just a lot of irresponsible young soldiers who've never really learnt their new jobs."

"If we haven't caught up with the bus by the time we get to Lubamba," Paul said, "we'll call the police from there."

They were passing through wooded country now. Tall trees, swathed in creepers, overhung the road. Once or twice Helena saw a monkey dart across it in front of the car. The road was a harsh red streak of dusty gravel, pitted with holes. Whenever they met a car coming in the other direction, the first they saw of it was a cloud of red dust and they hastily wound the windows up until it had passed. Even so, Helena could feel grit in her mouth and her eyes smarted.

Paul had been compelled to drive slower. But not much slower. He was forcing everything that he could out of the car and when they passed the rather quaint notices at the roadside which said "Be Aware of Flying Stones," he appeared to think that the flying stones might be dodged

if only he went ahead fast enough. But the time began to seem long to Helena. She began to feel that they would never catch up with the bus, would never get to Lubamba, perhaps were not even on the right road to it, had somehow become deeply lost in this strange, tropical country, in a problem that they had not even begun to understand.

Presently they were in open country, with low blue hills in the distance. There were fewer cottages, there was hardly anyone at the roadside, and there were not many trees standing in the hummocky brown grass, except for clumps of the African thorn, with their umbrellas of dark, spiney leaves and beautifully graceful, slender golden trunks, and an occasional erythrina, the tree that Helena had noticed on her first day in Uyowa, the flame-red blossoms of which made it look as if it were being consumed by fire.

Sometimes they caught a glimpse of a small gazelle, a few humpbacked oxen, a grove of papyrus or bamboo. At any other time Helena would have been deeply fascinated, but now she almost hated the unfamiliarity of it all. The most familiar thing was the sky, yet even it had its strangeness, the strange pallor and remoteness that made it peculiarly the sky of Africa.

When they saw the bus it was still some distance ahead of them. They could see a long way in that open country. The bus was only a small one, the kind that holds seven or eight people. They saw it only for a moment, then lost it behind some stony mounds. Then they saw it again, enveloped as they were themselves in a red-dust-cloud.

Paul gave a whoop and accelerated.

The car lurched strangely, jolted abnormally violently and slithered sideways in the dust. Paul jerked it to a standstill and jumped out. In helpless frustration he kicked at one of the tyres.

"A puncture!" he said in a desperate voice. "Now, holy God, we've got a puncture!"

The bus receded.

CHAPTER VI

Helena and Mr. Forrest got out on the other side of the car. The rear right-hand tyre was flat. Paul crouched down to look at it.

"We've picked up a nail," he said.

"It could have been something worse," Mr. Forrest said. "Let's get on with changing it."

Paul straightened and opened the boot.

For a moment he stood there, saying nothing, only staring into it. His father moved up behind him and looked over his shoulder. Then they exchanged a long look.

"What is it?" Helena asked. "What's wrong?"

"No spare wheel," Paul said.

She joined them quickly behind the car. In the boot she saw a cardboard box of beer bottles, another box containing some polythene-wrapped sandwiches, some other picnic gear, some books, a rug.

"Where is it then?" she asked.

"That's what we're wondering too," Mr. Forrest said.

"And when it was removed." Paul bent to look at the nail again. "You know, if we didn't simply pick this up, if it was driven in. . . ." He stopped and looked up at his father. Once more the two of them gazed at each other steadily.

Then, as if to rid himself of some hazy but ugly thought, Mr. Forrest said positively, "It wouldn't have lasted as long as this."

"It might have," Paul said, "if the nail only went through the outer casing. As a matter of fact, I've been feeling a slight drag on the steering for some time."

"I don't understand," Helena said.

"Nor do we," said Paul.

"You both look as if you think you do understand something I don't." She looked from one face to the other. "Do you think the spare wheel's been deliberately removed? Hasn't it just been left behind by mistake?"

"Yes, of course." Mr. Forrest agreed with her too readily.

"I'm sure that's what happened. The question is now, what do we do about it?"

"Get the wheel off, then I'll flag the next car that comes along," Paul said, "and try hitching a ride to that last village we passed. I saw a garage of sorts there. With luck they'll be able to help."

"It might be better to try to get a ride the other way into Lubamba," his father said. "Then, if you've missed the bus there, you could probably hire a car to follow them on."

"Suppose I can't get a car."

His father nodded, rubbing a hand reflectively up and down his jaw. "You may be right."

"Couldn't we split up?" Helena said. "Paul could go back to the garage in the village and I could go on to the hotel in Lubamba. Or I could stay here with the car, if you like, and Mr. Forrest could go on to Lubamba."

"No, I know what we'll do," Paul said. He had already taken the jack out of the car. "I'll take the first car that'll stop, which ever way it's going. Then I'll either go back to the garage and get them to fix the tyre—with luck that shouldn't take much over an hour—or I'll go on to Lubamba and see what I can organise there. At least I'll be able to telephone for a car from the hotel so that you're picked up."

"All right, but of course you may have quite a wait before anything comes along in either direction," his father said. "Meanwhile it would be sensible, I think, to move the car into that patch of shade. You could manage that, I expect."

"Yes, I——"

But Paul was already working on the jack and did not answer.

Only a few minutes after he had the wheel off a red cloud of dust appeared at the corner where they had last seen the bus and, without waiting for any more discussion, Paul stepped forward into the middle of the road with his arms out. The dust-cloud swept down on him with a great jangling of ancient machinery. The dust was enveloping Paul before the vehicle stopped, a bus itself, with a row of dark faces at the windows looking down at the three people in the road with placid curiosity.

Paul spoke to the driver who nodded and made a little gesture with his thumb for Paul to come aboard carrying the wheel that he had taken off the car. He got on to the step, turned to wave to Helena and his father, then disappeared inside. The clanking of machinery started up once more, the settling dust rose again and the bus drove on.

"Well," Mr. Forrest remarked, "I think it would have been sensible to get this into that patch of shade, it'll soon be an oven. Not that we need wait inside it, of course. But if you sit down on the ground, even on a rug, you tend to get eaten up by ants. There's nothing against stretching our legs when we feel like it, however."

"Mr. Forrest," Helena said, "will we ever catch that bus now? Really?"

"Oh, I'm sure we shall," he answered. "They'll take quite a time over their lunch in the hotel, then they'll go on on the usual route. We're absolutely certain to catch up with them sooner or later. Now what about having lunch ourselves? It's a bit early, perhaps, but it seems as good a time as we're likely to get."

"I think food would choke me."

Helena was already half-choking from the dust. It had coated her nostrils and her throat. When she blew her nose her handkerchief was stained red as if her nose were bleeding.

"Well, have a glass of beer, then," Mr. Forrest said. He opened the boot again, opened a bottle of beer and poured it into a plastic tumbler. "Tepid, unfortunately, but I expect it'll help. Drink it slowly. Now would you like a book to help pass the time? I've only got Gibbon here, I'm afraid. I always keep a few volumes of Gibbon in each of the cars. You can always open him anywhere and start reading and then stop without any undue irritation when it's possible to drive on again."

She shook her head, but took the tumbler and drank the half-warm, fizzy flui

The shade into which they had moved was not very deep.

It was cast by some tall, spindly trees that had no foliage except at the top, where it sprouted out in a few green tufts, which allowed a good deal of sunshine through to heat the little pool of shadow under them and speckle it with flecks of light.

Helena moved about restlessly, sipping the beer. The car was standing across the entrance to a sort of lane which ran in through the trees for about fifty yards to one of the round, thatched huts typical of the country. Two children had come out of the hut and were standing still there, observing her and Mr. Forrest and the car.

Mr. Forrest had taken one of his volumes of Gibbon out of the car and was holding the book in one hand, a plastic tumbler in the other and was sipping and reading.

She interrupted him, "You know what we ought to have done? We ought to have arranged with Paul that you and I should go on together to Lubamba when we get the chance, just leaving the car here."

He looked up from his book.

"Yes, that *is* what we should have done," he said. "Of course. Why didn't we think of it? The trouble is, I think so slowly nowadays. Senility puts a brake on the mind. Paul, on the other hand, who appears so level-headed, often acts so fast that he hasn't given himself adequate time to think a matter out."

"Well, couldn't we do it now, if a car comes along? We could leave a note for Paul tucked into the windscreen, telling him what we've done."

"The only thing wrong with that is that unfortunately the car might not be here when he got back."

"Do you mean it would be stolen?"

"All too probably. Either in one package, or piecemeal. I've a great liking for the local people, and a great regard too, but I can't blind myself to the fact that they're somewhat given to thievery. Who can blame them? They're so terribly poor. And the loss of the car wouldn't matter if it helped us to catch up with Jean. But Paul wouldn't get our message."

"No. I see. Then I suppose there's nothing to be done

but wait—unless I go on by myself and you stay here. Why shouldn't I do that?"

"No, I think not. No, definitely not."

"But why?"

"Because this isn't Kent or Sussex. And it happens that we're responsible for you here. No, I think we'll stick together. Once a plan's been made, in general I've a preference for sticking to it. It generally works out best."

His gentle tone admitted no argument. Helena understood why he had been a successful headmaster.

The two children from the hut were edging shyly nearer. Suddenly their shyness seemed to evaporate and they came bounding up to Mr. Forrest and Helena, stopping about two yards away and staring at them with broad smiles. The elder was a girl of about ten. She had on a brief little cotton dress, its colours faded by much washing. The younger was a boy of about eight, dressed in a little kilt of rags which was hung round his middle on a string. Both children had an air of wild, cheerful liveliness, yet their thin arms and legs and little pot bellies told the sad story of malnutrition.

Mr. Forrest spoke to them in their own language. The girl at once turned shy again and looked away. The boy answered, laughing.

"What did you say to them?" Helena asked.

"Oh, I only told them that our car has broken down and that we're waiting for help. The boy thinks it's very funny for a fine car like that to break down."

"Can they speak any English?"

"Try them."

She said to the children, "Do you speak any English?"

"Yes, yes, hallo," the boy said.

"How old are you?"

His eyes went evasive and he looked away.

"I think that's about all he knows," Mr. Forrest said. He spoke again in the children's language, and as before the boy answered.

Mr. Forrest translated for Helena. "I asked, is it far

to Lubamba? He said it was a long way, then that it wasn't. He isn't sure what I want it to be."

"Is it far?" she asked.

"I don't think so. Seven or eight miles, perhaps."

The boy came a step or two closer to Helena and looked up at her with bright, gently appealing eyes.

"Ten cents?" he murmured hopefully.

She was starting to open her handbag when Mr. Forrest stopped her.

"I shouldn't," he said. "Not yet. Wait till we're just leaving, or the word will go round and we'll be mobbed."

"But there's no one about to mob us," she said.

"That's what you think. But those ten cents might transform the very sticks and stones into little boys and girls with their hands out."

She closed her bag and shook her head at the boy.

He accepted it good-naturedly and strolled past her to take a look at the car, while the girl suddenly lost interest in them and scampered back to the hut. The boy examined the car carefully, then walked all round Mr. Forrest and Helena, then wanted to be shown the book that Mr. Forrest was reading. He held it out and the boy stared long and thoughtfully at a page of Gibbon.

"And now," Mr. Forrest said to Helena, "he's probably read as much of it as you ever have. But perhaps you'll both come to it some day."

He resumed his reading, while the boy, after again going all round the car, touching the figures on the number plate as if he were trying to make them out and drawing some zigzag lines in the dust on the bonnet, wandered back to the hut.

He emerged again later, once with his sister and once without her, and once with his father, a small wiry man in a ragged shirt and shorts. The man had come out to ask if they were all right or if there was any help that he could give them. He chatted to Mr. Forrest for some minutes, while Helena walked about, then sat down in the car, found it already too hot and got out and walked about again.

Presently she found that she could face the idea of a sandwich, and after that she found that it was easy to

eat two more. For some time no cars had passed in either
direction, then several went by within a few minutes of each
other. It would not have been difficult to get a lift. Helena
was tempted to suggest once more that she should, but almost
as if he had felt the suggestion coming, Mr. Forrest suddenly
began to read aloud.

" 'It was an ancient custom in the funerals, as well as in
the triumphs of the Romans, that the voice of praise should be
corrected by that of satire and ridicule, and that, in the midst
of the splendid pageants which displayed the glory of the
living or the dead, their imperfections should not be
concealed from the eyes of the world.' " He turned to
smile at Helena. "There now, wasn't that a good idea
they had? I've always liked it. I think it might be very
good for some public men to know that that was waiting for
them."

"I think it sounds hideously macabre," said Helena. "Who
wants a funeral to be fun?"

"Well, everyone except those immediately involved, and
they're generally a sadly small number."

She gave him a long stare. "I wonder," she said, "*are* you
quite heartless? Have you by any chance forgotten Jean?"

"Not for a moment."

"Then how can you read and joke like that?"

"It's just a habit. But I won't go on if it disturbs you."
He closed the book. "We might be discussing that spare
wheel, I suppose, and why it's missing. Yet we can't arrive at
anything by discussing it—not at the moment. We've got
to do some investigation first. But it happens, you see, that
my chauffeur, Erasmus, worships our two cars. He cleans
them, he tends them, as if they were his children. In my
hands or in Paul's a spare wheel could easily be mislaid,
but in those of Erasmus, no—no, really I don't think so.
Well, I won't say it isn't impossible for him to have made
a mistake, but I'll go as far as saying that it's in the
highest degree unlikely."

"So that's what you were thinking about while you were
pretending to read," Helena said. "It was about who landed
us out here like this."

"Oh, I wasn't pretending," he said. "I'm a person who has to keep occupied, reading, building pergolas, anything, or I tend to brood and dream in a very unprofitable way. About villages in Sussex, for instance, and primroses in the spring. Do you know, occasionally it strikes me as perfectly intolerable that I shouldn't have seen a primrose for years. I mean it literally, years. Because when we go to England for a visit, we naturally go in the summer, to avoid the more inclement weather. But I'm getting off the point and you'll be calling me heartless again in a minute. Tell me, can you make sense of what's happened? I mean, the removal of the spare wheel and the nail in the tyre suggest that we weren't meant to catch the bus. On the other hand, who'd kidnap a child on a bus? A tourist bus, at that. Unless it's the other way round, of course, and it's Jean who's kidnapped the woman. Jean, after all, couldn't drive a car, so it wouldn't be unreasonable to use a bus."

"Now you're being flippant again," Helena said.

"I'm sorry. I ought to add, however, that I'm perfectly aware Jean could be worth kidnapping. My wife is a rich woman."

"And you think it *is* kidnapping now," Helena said. "You and Paul. I saw how you looked at one another."

"I don't know, Helena, I don't know." He looked at his watch. "Paul's been gone an hour now. I hope he isn't much longer."

He was about twenty minutes longer. When he arrived it was in a lorry that was carrying crates of soft drinks to Lubamba. The driver of the lorry stopped to help Paul to replace the wheel, then started off, waving to them when the car passed him a minute or two later.

Paul drove really fast now, successfully avoiding any flying stones but not the potholes in the road. Helena slid low in her seat to avoid the feeling that at any moment she would be thrown against the roof of the car. In the time that he had been gone Paul seemed to have worked himself up into a state of rather dangerous excitement. From the way that his lips were drawn back, showing his teeth in a grimace that caricatured a smile, he looked as if he were actually enjoying the wild drive, the shuddering of the car and the sudden scattering of chickens and dogs as they roared through a village.

A mile beyond the village they came to the Lubamba Lakeside Hotel. One or two cars, but no buses, were standing before it. The hotel was a long white building, only one storey high, built at right-angles to the road, so that its terrace and most of its windows faced the lake. The lake was a shining stretch of water that wound away and disappeared between low rounded hills in a blue distance. Near the hotel the surface of the water was covered by a great carpet of pale pink water lilies.

"*Nelumbium niloticum*," Mr. Forrest observed as he and Helena waited on the terrace while Paul went striding into the hotel to find someone who could tell them how long the bus had been gone and if there had been a little girl of seven years old on it. "Pretty, isn't it?"

There was a dead tree, a grey wooden skeleton, standing up out of the midst of the water lilies. It looked like a strange ornament carefully placed on a delicate silken rug. Helena had already wondered at the number of dead trees that they had seen in the landscape. She had wondered if they were the tokens of some great fire that had swept across the country, or if, when a tree grew to a certain size here, it simply gave up and died.

Between the lakeside and the hotel the rough dry grass was starred with tiny flowers that seemed to bloom straight out of the red earth without any stem. Near the edge of the water a marabou stork, with its high-shouldered stoop and its drooping feathers giving it an air of shabby arrogance, picked its way among the water lilies.

When Paul emerged from the hotel entrance on to the terrace he brought a woman with him. She was about fifty, white, fat, ungirdled, dressed in old slacks that showed every line of her sagging body and a tight white shirt that gaped between the buttons, showing the sweaty flesh inside. She had artificially blonde hair and a good deal of powder on her pouchy, hard-eyed, authoritative face.

"Sorry," she said. "Sorry can't help you. Glad to if I

could, but not a thing I can do." Her eyes defied them to suggest that there was any way in which she might help. There was a strong smell of beer on her breath. "Best thing you can do is just keep going. Bus left half an hour ago."

"But the child," Mr. Forrest said. "Was there a child on it? Have you asked her that, Paul?"

"Yes," Paul said, "and she says there was."

"A small girl," Mr. Forrest said, "seven years old, dark haired, dressed in——" He turned to Helena.

"Blue jeans and a red blouse," Helena said.

"That's right," the woman replied. "Noticed her. Thought, nice kid, having the time of her life, nice to see it. Can't see there was any reason to suspect anything was wrong. Can't see you can blame me. Sorry and all that, of course, that I didn't catch on, but can't see it was my fault."

"No one's thinking of blaming you, madam," Mr. Forrest said. "We're only grateful for any information you can give us. Was the child with a woman?"

"I suppose so," the woman said. "Didn't notice particularly. Just one of the crowd to me. Have them through every day, you know, about seven on each bus. Can't possibly keep track of who belongs to who and so on. Just happened to notice the child because we don't have so many children through and, as I said, she was having the time of her life. Went down to try to talk to the old stork, and I had to send one of the boys after her to make sure she didn't go in the water. Bilharzia, of course. And that's all I can tell you. Don't see you can expect me to have noticed any more. Sorry."

"Well, at least it seems certain Jean is on the bus and so far has come to no harm," Mr. Forrest said.

"Harm?" The woman laughed a squelchy, drinker's laugh. "Having the time of her life. Time of her life, I told you."

"So we'll take your advice and get on after the bus," he said.

"You do that." She stumped back into the hotel.

The two men and Helena returned to the car and Paul drove on.

He drove as fast as before but Helena felt that, little as the woman had been able to tell them, he had slightly relaxed. At least they knew now that Jean was safe and for the present apparently enjoying herself. Somehow it began to seem credible that the nail in the tyre and the missing spare wheel had been accidents, and that Jean had simply beguiled some irresponsible person into taking her on the tour. And soon they would catch up with the bus, stop it and claim her.

"You know, when we get her back, I think we ought to take her on to see the elephants and the Falls," Mr. Forrest said presently, "so that she doesn't hate us all too much for rescuing her. We've just got to find a telephone somewhere and let Judy know that all's well."

"You were supposed to telephone from Lubamba," Helena reminded him.

"Quite right," he said. "I was. But in the circumstances I think it was more important to avoid delay. It might have taken quite a long time getting a call through to Tondolo."

"We could spend the night at the Ross Falls Lodge," Paul said, "and take Jean up the river to-morrow to see the hippos and the crocodiles, and drive home in the afternoon."

"Yes, that'll be pleasant for Helena too," Mr. Forrest said. "You'll be very interested, Helena, and with worry about Jean off your mind you'll be able to enjoy it all properly. I don't suppose you've enjoyed the drive very much so far."

"*Enjoyed?*" Helena began to laugh. If there was hysteria in it, at least it was the first laugh that had been heard in the car since they started out, and she was still laughing when the car came to a jolting halt, because half a dozen uniformed Uyowan soldiers were strung out across the road in front of it.

All except one carried rifles. That one held a sub-machine gun which he was pointing at Paul. The weapon looked old but serviceable and the face of the man holding it had a look of stolid ferocity. It wouldn't trouble him to shoot, even if he was not over-eager to do so. He was tall and unusually heavily built for a Uyowan. His uniform of khaki cotton was impeccably neat. He advanced to the side of the car and rested the gun on the frame of the window.

"Your travel permits, please," he said.

There was silence in the car.

He raised his voice to a curious falsetto. "Your travel permits!"

The silence, the shocked stillness, in the car continued for a moment longer. No one had thought of permits since they had started out. Then Paul put a hand in his pocket and brought out his wallet. He took out a note and held it out to the man. The man with the gun barely glanced at it as he took it.

"The others," he said. "There is a State of Emergency. No one may travel without travel permits. Your permits."

Paul took some more money out of his wallet and handed it over.

The big man hesitated, as if he were wondering if it were worth his while to extort more, then shrugged his shoulders and motioned the other soldiers to get out of the way.

"You must at all times be ready to show your travel permits," he said loudly. "It is for your own safety. There are bad people about."

Paul drove on. Looking back, Helena could see the soldiers lighting cigarettes and laughing.

"Expensive, but unavoidable," Paul said.

"Would they really have shot if you hadn't paid up?" Helena asked.

"Unlikely," he answered. "More probably we'd just have got bogged down in hours of argument. On the other hand, when a bunch of trigger-happy soldiers get loose here with no one in charge, you can never be quite sure where you are. D'you know, I've never once thought of those damned permits since we were questioning the clerk about who got them for the bus passengers. It never once entered my head that we might need them ourselves."

"Nor mine," his father said. "But it could have been worse. We didn't lose more than five minutes over it."

"I wonder what it takes to make you say that things couldn't be worse, Mr. Forrest," Helena said.

"Well, I believe in reserving one's emotions for the really big issues with which one occasionally has to deal," he said. "And in spite of that little delay we shall certainly catch up with the bus soon. Even if we don't manage it before they get to the Falls, we'll find them there, because they always stop there for quite a while, so that people can wander around and take photographs. They keep stopping in the Park too, so that people can photograph the animals. Oh, we'll catch them up any time now."

As he spoke, another khaki-clad figure moved out from the side of the road and waved to them peremptorily to stop.

This time, however, it was only a tse-tse fly control post and the man who inspected the car for the pest was quick, courteous and did not require to be bribed. But as he looked round the inside of the car, another man wandered out in front of it.

He was old, so old that his skin as well as his hair had changed from black to dusty-looking grey and he wore, besides his rags, the strangest hat that Helena had ever seen. It was made of a pair of immense buffalo horns somehow attached to his head by a piece of grimy felt, and it gave him an air of grotesque authority. Round his neck he wore with obvious pride a placard on which was written in shaky capitals, "I AM A BEGGAR NOT A THIEF."

Standing in front of the car, apparently oblivious of it yet blocking the way ahead, he seemed to be lost in some quiet dream, and as if he were ready to go on standing there till the dream had worked itself to an end. Paul gave him a few coins, the young guard put a hand on his shoulder, pulled him to the side of the road and Paul drove on.

Then he had to stop again at the Park entrance and pay to be let in. There was a notice just inside the entrance, which read, "Ross Falls National Game Reserve. Elephants Have The Right of Way."

Helena thought, "I should hope so." Even Paul in his present mood, she hoped, would not dispute the right of way with an African elephant.

As they drove on the road went steeply downwards into a broad, level valley. It was a strange, barren landscape, dotted everywhere with the grey skeletons of dead trees and the tall red cones of ant-hills. At first it all seemed lifeless. The rains, Helena had been told earlier, were late that year and the grass looked as bleached and dead as the trees. Then in the distance she saw movement, a small dark mass, like a shadow on the ground, that changed its shape as she watched.

"Buffalo," Mr. Forrest told her.

Then an animal that he told her was a hartebeest sprang across the road and went galloping into the distance and a moment afterwards Helena saw her first elephant. It was almost at the roadside, and was eating grass, pulling up tufts of it with the tip of its trunk and stuffing it into its mouth, tucking away every last blade with meticulous neatness. It watched the car with complete indifference.

After that there were more elephants, some alone, some in small herds. One group of four startled Helena into momentarily disbelieving what she was seeing because instead of being the usual dark grey mountains of muscle and bone, they were red. A strong, brick red.

"No!" she cried. "No! I have never, never in my life heard of a red elephant!"

"It's just that they like rolling in the ant-hills," Mr. Forrest explained. "They feel nice and scratchy, I suppose. I'm so sorry we can't stop so that you can have a better look at them. But we'd better press on."

"Since we haven't met the bus coming out," Paul said, "we can be pretty certain it's still at the Falls."

"So our troubles are nearly over," said his father.

"God, I hope so!"

Paul sounded as if he had passed the point of being able to believe that anything could go right.

But what could go wrong now, unless the woman in

the Lubamba hotel had lied to them about Jean having been with the bus party, and why should she do that?

They met only one car leaving the Game Reserve, and only a moment after passing it, they saw the bus. At the same moment Helena realised that a low and continuous noise of which she had been aware for the last few minutes was the roar of waters. The bus was parked on a flat patch of ground above the waterfall. The pale, glimmering, lacy curtain that tossed about lightly in the air beyond the bus was the spray rising a hundred feet above the river as it plunged down into its deep, narrow cleft.

The African driver of the bus was leaning against the bus, smoking. The passengers who had been looking at the Falls and photographing them were beginning to drift back to it. There was a big, pink-faced, bald man of about forty with a teutonic air about him. There was a plump woman of about fifty with curly, blued hair, who was wearing slacks and looking hot and tired and who could only have been American. There was a young Indian couple, the woman in a sari of heavy cinnamon-coloured silk. In spite of all its drapery about her ankles, she moved over the rough ground with easy elegance. There was a pale-faced, dark-haired young man who had so many strange pieces of photographic equipment attached to him by a leather strap that hung round his neck that they might have been charms. They looked magical, heathen.

There was no one else. There was no tall, blonde young woman in dark glasses. There was no Jean.

CHAPTER VII

The American woman was saying to the teutonic-looking man, "Well, I don't care if it isn't the Nile, it's a tributary of the Nile and to me it'll always be like the source, because it's the nearest I've seen with my own eyes."

With a heavy accent he replied, "But the source of the Nile is at Owen Falls in Uganda. There is a fine hydro-electric dam there. Believe me, I have seen it with *my* own eyes."

"Who wants the source of the Nile to be a fine hydro-electric dam?" she asked. "The Nile with all its history—Cleopatra and all. I came to Africa looking for romance and magic, not hydro-electric dams. We've got those back home. And I kind of like this place. It's got atmosphere."

The dark-haired young man, whose English revealed him to be a Frenchman, said, "It is regrettable it's not possible for you to go closer to the Falls. To see them from here is nothing, they merely vanish over the edge into a cloud of foam."

"Well, I'm quite satisfied with what I've seen," the woman said, "and I didn't even go near the edge. I've no head for heights."

Paul had stopped the car behind the bus and he, Helena and his father had got out.

They stood in silence on the patch of flat ground there, looking round. Helena was thinking that Jean and her companion, being young, might have wandered farther from the bus than the others and be taking longer to return. But there was only one direction in which they could have got out of sight of the rest. It was up a long flight of steps, close to the edge of the gorge, which led to the top of a small hillock. The steps were wooden and had once had a wooden handrail beside them. Now half the steps were missing and the handrail was broken. But still, an active child and a young woman could easily have scrambled up and if they had then walked on a little way along

D

the edge of the gorge, they would soon have become invisible from the bus.

The gorge was very narrow, and its sides, drenched with spray, shone in that arid country with a startling greenness. Trees that had sprouted out of mere cracks in the rock grew up its sides. Emerald mosses hung down covering the stone. The water itself was deeply green, under the dancing rainbows in the mist above it.

This was not one of the waterfalls that merely punctuate the movement of a great river, which flows in placid silence until it suddenly takes the great plunge downward. At Ross Falls three small rivers came together. All were narrow and shallow and ran playing and glittering over the stones in their beds until they met. Then immediately they hurled themselves down together into a cleft, no more than thirty feet across, to flow along in it, churning wildly, for half a mile, only then escaping as a wide calm river that continued for many miles.

A stretch of that distant calm could be seen from the plateau where the bus stood. The water was silver and blue and rose-pink with reflections of the sky and the sunshine. But to see far into the gorge was impossible. The sides were too steep and there were fences along the edge and notices that gave stern warning of the dangers of going beyond them. The fences were as broken down as the steps on to the hillock and the notices were only just legible, but why they were there was clear.

Helena was starting to walk towards the steps when Paul stopped her.

"Wait a minute. My father's going to make some inquiries. We may as well begin by finding out what we can."

Mr. Forrest went up to the driver of the bus.

"I believe you'd a little girl and a young woman travelling together on your bus to-day." His voice gave away almost nothing of his anxiety, for he was taking pains not to put the man on the defensive. "Do you know where they are now?"

The driver counted his flock. "Somewhere," he said. "Looking at the Falls. They come soon. I tell them we stay here half an hour, not more."

"But they were on your bus, were they?" Mr. Forrest said. "They came all the way here with you?"

"Yes, yes." The driver ground out the stub of his cigarette in the dust at his feet. "You friends of theirs? They come now."

He made it sound as if he saw them coming. But in fact Jean and the young woman were nowhere in sight.

"They went up there, perhaps," Mr. Forrest said, gesturing at the steps.

The American woman broke in, "That's right, they did, I saw them. I saw them climbing up and I thought, 'I believe I'll try that myself,' but when I got close and saw how steep and broken down the steps were, I thought 'No, don't you do that, you just be content with looking at the Falls from here,' so that's what I did."

"I'd like to make sure that we're talking about the same little girl and young woman," Mr. Forrest said. "The child is seven, and she's got short dark hair and was wearing blue jeans and a red shirt."

"Yes, and she was just the cutest little thing you ever saw," the woman said. "She knew so much about everything. I declare she was the only one of us who knew the difference between a wildebeest and a hartebeest." Her friendly blue eyes, dwelling on the old man's face, grew troubled. "Is there something wrong? I can't imagine it. She was just so happy."

"Thank you—I hope not," he answered.

By then Helena had again started towards the steps, and this time Paul followed her.

At the top the noise of the water seemed even louder than it had from below and they could see more of its glassy green sweep as it poured over the rock-edge facing them into the chasm.

"There's no one here," Paul said.

"No," Helena agreed.

But the sense of all the roaring power down there under the airy veil of spray was having a peculiar effect on her, and she had hardly looked round. She felt the depths pulling her towards them, taking an irresistible hold on her. It was a sickening and frightening sensation. She wanted to throw herself on the ground and dig her fingers into the grass to fight the power. Instead she grasped Paul's arm.

He glanced at her face and said, "Not good at heights? Let's get farther back."

He led her farther away from the edge.

"Thanks," she said. "I'm sorry. Heights don't usually upset me." She took a long look round.

They could see for a great distance over the dry grassy country. There were occasional clumps of small bushes here and there and the usual dead trees. One of these, not far away, had a fish eagle sitting motionless on one of its topmost branches. Against a slope a long way off a dark patch stirred slightly. Buffalo, again, Helena thought, or perhaps elephants. They were too far away to be sure. A few immense, deep clouds moved very slowly in the pale sky.

"But what can have happened to them?" she asked. For some reason she found herself whispering.

Paul stood there looking unusually helpless and uncertain. His rather thorny self-confidence had suddenly left him. He turned towards the roaring of the Falls.

"God, Helena, I'm scared!" he said.

Just then the driver of the bus and the young Frenchman appeared at the top of the steps. The driver looked round, then disappeared again. The Frenchman came towards them. With camera in one hand and all the equipment slung round his neck, he looked a very witch-doctor of photography.

"Not here?" he said, surveying the empty scene. "But they were here. I was up here myself, taking photographs. I saw them. It is very strange."

"You definitely saw the child and the young woman up here?" Paul asked.

"Yes, together, looking at the waterfall."

"How long ago?"

"Ten minutes. A quarter of an hour. They must be near."

"Where?"

The Frenchman frowned at the distance. Then he walked to the very edge of the cliff and stood looking down.

"No, they could not have climbed down here. That is impossible. And for the moment I do not see them anywhere else." He turned back. "But may I ask what has happened? Why you worry? They appeared very content with one another. They were enjoying the trip together."

"Can you tell us anything about the woman?" Paul asked. "She appears, you see, to have taken it into her head to bring the child on this tour without consulting her family. We don't know who she is or anything about her."

"Ah! Now I understand. I wish I could help. But no, there is not much I can tell you. She was tall and slender, with a very fine, clear skin. Fair-haired, I think, but she wore a silk head-scarf all the time, and I do not know the colour of her eyes, because she wore dark glasses even at lunch in the hotel. She said she had come from England on a holiday to friends in Tondolo and the little girl was their granddaughter."

"Did you notice what name the child called her by?" Paul asked. "It wasn't mummy, or mother, or Marcia, by any chance?"

Helena gave Paul a quick glance. She remembered how he had mocked his mother when she had suggested that the unknown woman could be Marcia Forrest, come to reclaim her child.

The Frenchman shrugged his shoulders. "I am sorry. I do not pay much attention. I am very much occupied with my photography. I am on a business trip to East Africa from Paris. I have only a few days in Uyowa, then I go to Kenya. I come on this trip for the pictures only, not the company."

"Well, they aren't up here," Paul said. "We may as well go back to the others."

But he did not move, except to look round once more at the empty landscape. Nothing stirred in it. Even the eagle on its high perch was as still as if it were part of the tree.

"Let's go," Helena said after a moment.

Unwillingly, they started back towards the top of the steps.

As they went, Paul asked the Frenchman, "Did anyone else in your party come up here—the Indian or the German?"

"The Norwegian? He is a Norwegian, also on business like me," the Frenchman said. "No, none of them came up here. The steps, as you see, are difficult. There was another man up here, but not of our party."

"Another man?" Paul said.

"Yes."

"Where did he come from? How did he get here?"

"He had a car. A grey Vauxhall. It was there." The Frenchman pointed to the right, at a point about ten yards from the edge of the cliff. "I do not know how he got it there. I think perhaps there is a way you can drive off the road somewhere and come straight here."

Paul went to the spot at which the Frenchman was pointing.

"Yes, here are his tyre-marks," he said. "And you can see them going this way. . . ." He started to follow them across the dusty grass. But suddenly he paused, turned and came back. "Helena, do you remember the car we met driving out of the Park?"

She nodded.

"Who was in it?" he asked.

"Just a man, I think," she said.

"Alone?"

"I think so."

"That's what I thought. I wonder if we could have been wrong."

The Frenchman went on, "He and his car were a nuisance to me. I did not want them in my pictures of the Falls, but it was very difficult to miss them. I waited, hoping he would leave, but he sat in his car, smoking and doing nothing, as if he would wait all day. In the end I did what I could and went back to take some pictures from above the Falls."

"Did you see him drive away?" Paul asked.

"No, from down there I think you would not see him. If he drove to join the road over there, I think no one in our party but me would have seen him at all." He pointed at where the road on which they had come curved back into view round the hillock.

"Except the child and the woman," Paul said.

"Yes, certainly, the child and the woman."

"Did they go to the car—talk to him—seem to know him?"

The Frenchman shrugged his shoulders. "I think not. But if they did, perhaps—no, I think not. But if they did, it is entirely possible I should not notice, unless they obstructed the view. I was very much occupied with my photography."

"I suppose they *didn't* obstruct it," Helena said. "I mean, you didn't accidentally get a photograph of any of them?"

The young man looked shocked at the suggestion that anything could possibly occur accidentally when he was taking a photograph.

"No, no," he said, "of that I am certain. I am sorry, it would give me the greatest satisfaction to be able to help you, I understand very well your grave concern, but I was most careful not to include the car or any of the people in my pictures. They were of no interest to me, you understand. I am a serious photographer, not one for taking snapshots of everyone I meet."

"Can you tell us anything about the man?" Paul asked.

"Only that he sat there in the car, smoking, and would not move."

"Can't you say if he was big or small, dark or fair, old or young?"

"He had a hat on," the Frenchman said, "a hat such as many of the Africans wear—cotton, with a brim drooping over his face. And dark glasses, like all of us. But he was not an African, he was white. And I think he was not very young. Not old, but not young."

"I see," Paul said. "Well, many thanks for your help. We'd better tell my father all this, then decide what to do next."

Again they went to the steps.

The party below were in a group round Mr. Forrest. They stood close together, as people will when they have been infected by a mood of anxiety. As the three from above scrambled down and joined them, the group opened up a little to include them, yet remained close, as if this would help to ward off some danger that threatened them all.

The Norwegian was just remarking sombrely, "Oh yes, I have heard it. Many people throw themselves in the river at this point. For some reason, it has great attractions for suicides."

"Quite true," the Indian said. "This is quite true. It is a well-known fact. Only a few months ago the body of a poor Sikh was discovered below the Falls—what had been left by the crocodiles."

"Well, I don't think it's at all kind of you to talk about it like that!" cried the American woman. "Not with these poor people here going just crazy with anxiety about their little girl. I'm sure you can't be right. If we just wait here a little, you'll see, she and her friend will come strolling along as if nothing had happened."

"It seems there's something else that may have happened to them, besides falling into the river," Paul said. He turned to the Frenchman. "Would you mind telling my father about the car you saw up there?"

The Frenchman described the car and what he could remember of the man who had been inside it.

Paul went on, "And I think we should get moving fast now, following that car we saw leaving the Park just after we came in, because that must have been the one."

"But there was only one person in that car," Mr. Forrest said.

"Can we really be sure?"

"I think so," his father said. "It was the man this gentleman's just described. You were driving, so perhaps you didn't take much notice of him, but I saw him clearly, and there was no one with him."

"Well then, what do we do?" Paul asked.

The driver of the bus ground the end of another cigarette into the dust. "I know what I have to do. I have to take my passengers to the Ross Falls Lodge, where they spend the night, and there I telephone my company that two passengers have got themselves lost. That is my responsibility. So, if you all please, get into your seats and we drive on."

"Just a minute," Mr. Forrest said. "I'm quite sure that's

what you must do, but if you don't mind, I'll come with
you. It's obvious now that I must get in touch with the police
as quickly as possible, and I could do that from the Lodge.
But my son and Miss Sebright will stay here with the
car, just in case this kind-hearted lady is right and my granddaughter and her companion come strolling along out
of the blue."

"There's no point in staying here. We ought to follow
that car," Paul said.

"The police are the people to chase that car, if it really
has anything to do with the case."

"If you can get them moving."

"I will, don't worry."

Mr. Forrest climbed into the bus after the other passengers.

When it had gone Helena and Paul stood for a while
looking silently at the tumbling, sparkling waters that came
together above the Falls. A small tree, vividly green, but
bent by the drift of the spray, grew up out of the middle
of one stream. A few big rocks jutted up here and there above
the foam. The air was full of the sound of water, the light,
rippling sound of the three streams a treble to the bass
roar of the waterfall. And yet, as soon as the rattling of
the bus had faded, Helena felt as if she were in the midst
of a deep silence.

She went to what was left of a wooden bench, facing the
junction of the streams, and sat down.

"They're letting everything go here, aren't they?" she
said. "The railings, the steps, this bench—all crumbling
away."

"Yes," Paul said, "that was to be expected. And it'll go a
lot farther before it stops. But why not? They may not
really like railings and steps and benches, and they've got
to find their own way of doing things. Helena——" He
moved to stand in front of her. "The woman that man
described *could* have been Marcia."

"I only wish she were," Helena said. "Then we'd have
nothing to worry about."

"I suppose you could say that. It would mean that Tean
was safe. But it wouldn't tell us who the man in the car was."

She thought about it for a moment, then she said, "It could have been someone she'd hired to drive her back."

"Why not go back in the bus?"

"The bus is going to a hotel, to spend the night. But if Marcia and Jean went straight back to Tondolo by car, they could get there by the evening, couldn't they, and catch a night flight back to London?"

He gave her a look of surprise. "D'you know, that almost makes sense."

"Except that it doesn't explain why they took the bus in the first place, or why they left it so secretly, in a way that was bound to worry everybody. Marcia has every right to take Jean home, if she wants to. She could have walked openly into your home and demanded her back. I imagine she'd have had a fight with your mother on her hands, but really none of you could have stopped her doing what she wanted."

"Except perhaps Jean herself."

"Jean?"

"Yes, why not Jean? Suppose Marcia did walk into our house last night when we were all at that party. Suppose she was all set to take Jean home straight away, but Jean said no. Jean said she wouldn't go till she'd seen some elephants. She said she'd been promised elephants. She went into a tantrum. I've never seen Jean in a tantrum, but I imagine she could make a pretty good thing of it. So Marcia bribed her into going quietly by promising her a trip to a Game Park first."

"That still doesn't explain why they came by bus instead of by car, if they could arrange for a car to meet them here."

"No." He sat down beside her. "All the same, how I wish it were true."

She gave an unhappy laugh. "While your father and I were waiting for you to come back with the tyre, he suggested it was really Jean who'd kidnapped the woman, and they came by bus simply because Jean couldn't drive."

Paul's head jerked round. His eyes were wide and startled. For a moment Helena thought he must imagine that she was serious. Then his look of surprise faded and left no expression of any kind on his face. It was as if a shutter had come down over it.

She said hesitantly, "Of course, as I've told you, I don't think—I've never thought—that Denis sent Jean out here without Marcia knowing all about it. So why, apart from anything else, should Marcia come rushing out to fetch her home?"

He stirred on the bench beside her, which sagged creakingly under his weight. Staring at the little tree bending in the stream, he said, "I'm a fool. I've been a fool about a lot of things. I haven't been thinking. I haven't really been thinking about anything but getting away. Now of course I'll have to put that off until Jean's found." Dropping his head into his hands, he shut his eyes, as if he were blotting out some intolerable vision.

"Will it really be so terrible, having to stay on for a time?" Helena asked, puzzled.

"Not that—no, of course not."

"Is it something to do with Cleo Grant then?"

He raised his head quickly and she thought that she saw something like terror in his eyes. "Why d'you ask that?"

"Only because your mother thinks she's the real reason why you want to go."

"Oh, that." He gave a short laugh. "My mother doesn't understand anything—anything at all. I was rather in love with Cleo once. She lived with us for some months, you know, after her parents died, and my mother had the whole thing fixed up in her own mind before Cleo had been two days in the house. But we got to know each other pretty well, Cleo and I, and I've always known that in a sense she isn't a real person. That's because there's only one human being who's ever meant anything real to her and that's Petrzelka, the man who left her flat when he found she hadn't any money. Everything about her after that happened, except for that awful need she had for him, turned into a sort of deception."

"What was he like, this Pet-something person?" Helena asked.

"Petrzelka. I didn't know him. It all happened in Kenya,

where her parents died. And you can never believe quite the whole of anything Cleo tells you. She doesn't exactly mean to lie, but she deludes herself. I remember she said Petrzelka was handsome and strong and brilliant and witty and every other damned thing, but I don't know if he was or not."

"At least to Cleo he was."

"You can't even be quite sure of that. She was working very hard, poor girl, to save her pride, and taking the line that he was quite right to leave her because with a brilliant career ahead of him, he couldn't afford to have a millstone like her round his neck. It's an odd thing, but it seems that if you abase yourself enough, you don't feel humiliation as frightfully as if you stand up on your own feet to take it."

"And has he had a brilliant career?"

"Not that I ever heard. I believe he went off to a job of some sort in the Congo. He was stateless, a refugee, which made things pretty tough for him, I expect, though I think it was part of why he so attracted Cleo. She loves other people to be lame ducks, dependent on her in one way or another. It makes her feel important." He turned to look at her curiously. "Why are you asking all this?"

"I suppose to pass the time."

"Well, it looks as if we may have a good deal of it to pass." He stretched out his legs and leant back, forgetting that the back of the bench had crumbled away. Only just saving himself from toppling backwards, he went on, "I suppose Cleo told you a good deal about us all before you came out here."

"She told me a certain amount."

"What did you make of what she said?"

"Only that you were all very wonderful. She said that repeatedly and I think she meant it. And I think she said you yourself had always been a contrary sort of character, and you must admit she's got something there."

"Has she? I don't see it myself. I always feel I'm a good deal more reasonable and consistent than most of the people I have to deal with."

"I'd call that a dangerous feeling."

"All the same, about this going back to England, for instance——"

"Oh, don't think I think there's anything contrary about that," Helena said. "I think you're probably right to go while the going's good."

"Well, that's pleasantly different from what I usually have to listen to here," he said. "It's generally taken to be a sign of incipient insanity to prefer the thought of harder work, less pay, a fairly unspeakable climate—and a wife, if I ever have one, who doesn't mind the idea of doing the cooking—to conditions here. To me it seems simple foresight. We don't belong here, we never have, we never shall. We're an utter irrelevance on the whole continent of Africa."

"What about the Indians?" she asked. "They don't belong here either."

"Ah, that's different," he said. "I'm damned sorry for them. Their lives are much more genuinely merged into the life of the whole community than ours have ever been. You won't find they've got day-dreams of villages in Sussex —or those villages to go to. And they're the professional people and the middlemen, the bankers, the shopkeepers, against whom hungry people naturally nurse a pretty fierce grudge. I shouldn't much care to be an Indian, living here nowadays. Now tell me what you yourself think about us all, Helena."

"You? Your family, d'you mean? You've all been extraordinarily kind to me."

"Yes, yes, we're hospitality itself—the fine old colonial tradition. But as separate people. You arrive here out of the blue and you've been going around in your quiet way for the last few days, judging us all. And my guess is the judgement isn't honestly very favourable."

"You have to remember, of course," she said, "that I was considering you as my future in-laws."

"Don't you think we might forget that?" he said.

"Are you sure you want to forget it?"

"I'm most horribly sure of it—abysmally shame-facedly sure of it."

"Do some more guessing then," she suggested. "What do do you think I think?"

He considered the question. "I think you'd put it far more politely, but that really you see my mother as a strong, selfish, possessive woman, remarkably unscrupulous in the way she goes about achieving anything she's set her heart on. I think you probably see my father as a charming old man, but essentially frivolous and self-deluding. That cottage in Sussex that he yearns for, for instance. He doesn't really want it. He'll tell you it's my mother who couldn't stand the life there, but it's he who couldn't. He couldn't bear to tear himself away from the place where he's really amounted to something in his time, to become a nobody in an England he wouldn't even recognise nowadays. Besides, he really loves the people here, you know, and a few of them even love him back. That's a lot to give up. Denis—you like Denis. That dithery charm of his worked on you like magic. And you'd have liked me far better if I'd been another edition of the same thing. But you think I'm evil-tempered and suspicious, probably with a neurotic thing about my mother—because of course you've realised she's at least half the reason why I'm going to England. If I don't get away from her, I'll be done for. I love her, but she wants to eat me up."

"And of course you know that you're simply putting all your own opinions on to me," Helena said.

"Nevertheless, isn't that more or less what you think?"

"Oh yes, but it happens to be only half the story. I think your mother's probably extremely generous and courageous and would face anything that she really had to, even that cottage in Sussex. I think your father's very kind and patient, and probably a great man in his way. I like Denis, as you said, but I don't think that was just because of some magic he used. And you. . . ." She drew an arc in the dust with the point of her shoe and stared down at it. "I think you're every bit as shy as Denis, just as afraid of your own feelings, but you act up aggressively instead of stammering and dithering. And besides that I think you're hiding something."

He seemed to shrink from her a little, then asked with false casualness, "Who isn't?"

She looked up at him. "But I mean, something special, Paul. I've seen how you and your father looked at one another once or twice to-day. There's something about what's happened that you understand, or think you understand, and you haven't wanted me to realise it. I believe you think you know what's happened to Jean."

"I don't," he said. "It's true I've a sort of private nightmare that's been growing on me all day—Josiah lying to us this morning—the spare wheel being missing—a kidnapping by bus—it all adds up———"

He stopped at the sound of a motor in the distance and stood up quickly as another car drove up and stopped behind their own.

A man and a woman got out, strolled about, took photographs, considered scrambling up the steep steps, decided against it, got into their car again and drove away.

When they had gone Paul did not return to what he had been saying, and as if to make sure that Helena would not press him to do so, said, "I think I'll take another look up there. Not that there's much point in it," and climbed the steps and disappeared.

While he was gone another car drove up and a party of four got out, looked at the Falls, took photographs and drove away. Later, after Paul had returned and sat down again on the bench beside Helena, there were other tourists. For Helena the tension grew all the time, bringing with it first restlessness, then a sense of aching exhaustion. Every time that she heard a car approaching she started to hope that it was Mr. Forrest returning with the police. When she saw only more tourists she came near to crying in desperation.

"I don't know why we stayed here," she said desperately when one party had just gone. "We aren't doing any good."

Paul picked up one of her hands. He held it rather awkwardly for a moment, as if he wanted to comfort her but did not quite know how.

"We know now it isn't any good, but it just might have been," he said. "Somebody had to stay."

"How much longer is it going to be?" she demanded tautly. "I believe you ought to have gone instead of your father. He's old. I don't believe he ought to have come at all. It's probably all too much for him."

"Don't worry about that. He's tougher than he looks, and much better than I am at dealing with the local people. He can always get them to do what he wants, where I'm only good at putting backs up. The police will be here soon."

"And what good can they do then? You were right, we ought to have followed that car."

"Perhaps. But you were both so sure there was only the one man in it."

"If they *weren't* with him . . ."

"Yes," he said as she stopped. "I know. Then they went over the edge."

That brought back silence.

Mercifully, soon afterwards, the car with Mr. Forrest and the police in it arrived.

They were a sergeant and a constable from some village nearby, tall, dark men in khaki uniforms with round black caps on their heads. Each had a truncheon and a revolver in a holster slung from his leather belt. They were slow-moving men, rather casual in their manner, almost as if this were routine, as if it had all happened before. And it soon became evident that, in their opinion, it had.

"Very bad place this," the sergeant said when he and the constable had walked along the river bank, climbed the steps, looked over the edge into the cauldron below and examined the tyre tracks and the ground round about for any other traces there might be of what had happened. "People come here, vanish, all the time. Nothing to do but drag river down there." He pointed towards the quiet expanse of water beyond the ravine, which was beginning to shine with fiery opalescence from the setting sun. "Bodies washed up always in one place. Easy to find but very dangerous for diver because of crocodiles. To-morrow—I think to-morrow we drag river. Nothing else to do. You go to the hotel now and to-morrow we tell you what we find."

"But the car, the man in the car?" Helena said. "Hasn't anything been done to find him?"

"The men at the tse-tse fly control post have been questioned," Mr. Forrest answered. "They remembered the car clearly and one of them, as usual, looked inside. And he's quite certain there was just one man in the car and no one else. Incidentally, I've telephoned Judy, and the sergeant's been on to the police in Tondolo. He's really a very good man, and he's quite right that there's nothing for us to do now but go to the hotel and wait. Come along. We may as well try to get there before dark." His face was a yellowish grey from fatigue as he shepherded Paul and Helena to the car.

They were stopped again themselves at the tse-tse fly control post. It was twilight by then. The beggar in his fantastic hat and flapping rags was still at the roadside, looking in the dusk like the priest of some ancient and barbaric religion. The young man who checked the car for the tse-tse fly shone an electric torch round inside it, wished them good evening and waved them on. The dark closed in on them quickly. Paul drove without haste now, almost as if he did not want to reach the hotel, where the three of them would have to mingle with other people, answer excited questions, accept sympathy. But at last it was there ahead of them, the lights from its windows reflected in the still water of the river.

Paul turned the car in beside the bus which they had chased so uselessly for so much of the day, and switched off the engine.

"Has it struck you," he said, "that they didn't look inside our boot at that control post? They looked round inside the car, but not in the boot. So perhaps they didn't look into the boot of that other car either."

There was silence for a moment. Then his father exploded, "Good God, Paul, you couldn't jam two people into the boot of a car—even if one was a child!"

"Not two people," Paul said, "but one you could. And if there was one—which was it?"

CHAPTER VIII

The hotel was a sprawl of single-storey buildings, looking in the dark more like a huddle of cottages than a hotel. Each cottage contained several rooms, with doors opening out on to a wooden verandah that ran the length of the building. The rooms were comfortably furnished, each with its own bathroom. There was a large cockroach in Helena's bath, but the porter who carried in her little overnight bag removed it for her.

He wore a tarboosh and a white cotton tunic and trousers piped with emerald green. The red of the tarboosh, the white and the bright green were all in vivid contrast to the man's deep brown skin. As she drank thirstily from a bottle of water labelled "Boiled and Filtered," Helena wondered wearily how so-called white skin had ever achieved its high reputation, when so-called black skin set off all other colours so much more splendidly.

She was very tired, her mind was muzzily confused, she felt slightly sick, and for the first time since coming to Uyowa she found the heat oppressive. That was the result of being so close to the river. The air was very humid, instead of dry and fresh as it was in Tondolo. She had a bath and emerged from it feeling slightly better, but she had to put on again the sticky clothes that she had worn all day and when she combed her hair she could feel the gritty dust clinging to it. If she were to wash it, she thought, red mud would pour out.

Joining Mr. Forrest and Paul in the bar, she drank two whiskies, which made the muzziness in her head worse but got rid of the nausea. Under quiet pressure from Mr. Forrest, who himself ate a good meal, she ate more than she had thought would be possible. Only Paul touched hardly anything, though the food was excellent. He had withdrawn completely into himself. When his father spoke to him he did not answer, and when the big Norwegian and the

American woman who had been on the bus, came up to ask if they had had any news of the missing child, Paul looked straight through them, much as Jean herself might have done when troubled by unwanted questions.

The bus party appeared to have had enough of one another's company for the day and had split up to sit at different tables. The American woman disturbed the dining-room in the middle of dinner by suddenly giving a loud shriek, but it was only because a bat had fallen out of the rafters into a bowl of fruit salad. Immediately after dinner Helena said good night to the two men and went back to her room.

She slept badly, dreaming of a red road that went on and on for ever across an empty desert, a desert that was like the most ancient of faces. But the red of this road was crimson, instead of the brick colour of the murram roads on which they had travelled all day, so that it looked like a trickle of blood making its way over an eternity of sad brown wrinkles. There was extreme terror in the dream, although nothing much happened.

Perhaps it was that nothing that was terrifying, the waiting and dreading and arriving nowhere. She woke shivering in the oppressive heat and was too scared for a time to try to go to sleep again.

She did sleep presently, only to wake again in renewed panic at a violent pounding on her door. But once she was fully awake she realised that the pounding was only a normal knocking and when she opened the door she found a waiter there with her morning tea. Glad that the night was over, even if the day to come were to turn out no better than the last, she drank the tea and got dressed and went looking for Paul and his father.

They were at breakfast already, engaged in a low-voiced conversation which they broke off as soon as they saw her.

"There's no news yet," Paul told her.

"Not even of the car?" she asked. "Have they tried to trace it?"

"They've tried, but they haven't found it."

"Have they really tried?"

"I think they're doing their best."

"What about those soldiers who stopped us?" she asked. "Didn't they see it?"

"I'm afraid if they accepted the same kind of travel permit as they did from us, they aren't going to admit it," Mr. Forrest said. He went on to order breakfast for Helena, then turned to her with a wary look as if he were afraid of the effect on her of what he was about to say. "I don't think the police are very interested in the car, you know. They're sure there was just the one man in it and they think he was probably an ordinary tourist who drove off the road where he did to avoid the crowd from the bus. What they're concentrating on is dragging the river below the Falls. There's this place where they say bodies get washed up. There's a diver working there now."

"The place with the crocodiles, the dangerous place," she said.

"It's all dangerous," Paul said. "There are crocodiles all the way along the river here."

"But if it's any comfort to you," Mr. Forrest said, "if it makes the thing a little easier to think about—anyone who went over the edge up by the Falls would be killed instantly on the rocks below."

"But why should they go over?" she cried. "Both of them. Has anyone come up with any answer to that yet? Both of them, I mean. If the woman had her reasons for throwing herself over, why should she take Jean too?"

"Perhaps it was Jean who went too near the edge and slipped and the woman tried to save her," Mr. Forrest said.

"I hadn't thought of that. . . ." She drank some of the coffee that had been brought to her. "What are we going to do?"

"The police want us to stay here while the diving operations are on, in case they find anything," Mr. Forrest said. "It would be a matter of identification, you see."

"Would there be anything left to identify?"

Paul stood up so abruptly that his chair fell over.

"I'm going to see if I can get a boat to take me up the

river to see what's going on," he said. "You can go with me or stay here, whichever you like."

His father said quickly, "I've got to stay here and I can't believe Helena has any desire at all to see what's going on."

"I'd have thought she might find it less of a strain than this sheer waiting," Paul said. "Anyway, I'm going to see what I can arrange. You can make up your mind about it while I'm gone, Helena."

He left them.

As he went Mr. Forrest gave an exhausted sigh and Helena realised that undoubtedly he had slept even less than she had.

She said, "I suppose you've cabled Denis, Mr. Forrest."

"No," he said, "not yet."

"You *haven't?*"

"No, we discussed it and decided to wait till we know something more definite."

"But you know something definite now—that Jean's disappeared."

"Well, we decided to wait at least until they give up the diving, or there's some news of that man in the car."

"So you *are* still thinking about him, even if the police aren't."

"We're trying to think of everything," he said.

But there was no hope on his face and for once he did not say that things might be worse than they were.

Paul came back after about twenty minutes, saying that he had arranged for a launch to take them up the river. Helena had decided to go with him. He and she went down together to the riverbank, then had to wait an infuriatingly long time while the man who had agreed to take them up the river tinkered dreamily with his motor, which he said was giving trouble. They waited in the shade of a sausage tree, as grotesque a tree as Helena had ever seen. Rows of salami-shaped fruits dangled on thin strings from all its branches, so that it looked like a mad sort of delicatessen, dumped down there to cater to the wayfarer in the bush. Paul fidgeted with impatience, saying that the man was going to take all day and that probably they might as well go back to the hotel. But at last the motor shuddered into life, the man beckoned them on board and the launch started slowly and noisily up the river.

It was wide here and flowed very quietly, very gently. There was no wrath or wildness in it. Yet it was not a kindly river. In the grass on the banks lay the long, armoured shapes of countless crocodiles, with their great jaws gaping, showing the bright yellow of their throats. Most of the trees growing close to the water were the usual grey, skeleton, dead things of this landscape, and every one of them had the sinister, hunched shape of a fish eagle on the topmost branch, waiting for prey. Only about the hippopotami there was an air of drowsy innocence. The huge creatures looked as if they had no evil designs on anything. When the launch came too close to them for the peace of their puzzled minds, they clumsily submerged, leaving only a pair of ears, nostrils and worried, bulging eyes showing above the water.

Standing stolidly in a pool at the water's edge a family of three watched the launch approach. There were two massive parents and their little one, which was exactly like them except in size. It looked like a toy, charmingly caricaturing them in miniature. Suddenly the noise and the smell of the launch overwhelmed it with panic. It tried to plunge under the water of the pool. But the pool was too shallow. Terrified, the young thing floundered helplessly till one of its parents thrust its immense muzzle down to comfort and reassure its child. Helena would never have believed till she saw it that the great bulk of a hippopotamus was capable of expressing such tenderness.

A little farther on she saw another sight which made her feel that at times the animal kingdom compares only too favourably with the human. A hippopotamus, a crocodile and a heron were peacefully sharing a pool. None was troubling the other. The hippopotamus stared stolidly at the launch, not yet nervous enough to plunge into deeper water. The crocodile lay at the edge of the pool, with its yellow throat exposed as if in a long-lasting, uncontrollable yawn. The heron, with exquisite grace, picked its way delicately through the shallow water.

But suddenly the illusion of peaceful co-existence was shattered. After all, this was not a place where the struggle to survive could ever be forgotten. The heron had strayed nearer than was wise to the crocodile. The murderous jaws snapped. With a squawk of terror and only just in time, the heron leapt away to safety.

The sly-looking ferocity of the crocodiles filled Helena with peculiar horror. She thought, "There's some poor devil of a diver down in this river now, looking for Jean and that woman. . . ."

But she and Paul never reached the point where the diving was going on. When Ross Falls, ahead of them, was still only a thin, silver streak drawn down the shadowy green of the ravine, they saw a launch coming towards them. There were several men in it, one of whom was waving at them.

It was the sergeant whom they had seen the evening before. "Stop!" he shouted. "Stop please! Stop! Wait!"

"Oh God, they've found them," Paul muttered, and Helena felt a shaft of ice go through her body.

The police launch came alongside and the sergeant and one other man climbed over on to the hired launch. The sergeant was carrying something, a smallish parcel done up in a sheet of plastic. His manner was as casual as it had been the evening before, except that he was smiling slightly, as if with satisfaction at some achievement. He sat down on one of the cross-benches under the canvas canopy and began to open the parcel.

"We have found something," he said. "Our diver, a very brave man, has been down three times without finding anything, then he has gone down again and this time he has found something. I brought it for you to identify."

His strong brown hands, with their pink fingernails and pink palms, carefully folded back the plastic.

Paul was standing nearer to him than Helena. He saw what was in the bundle before she could, turned, gripped her by the arms and spun her round so that she found herself staring up the river again towards the silver streak of the waterfall.

"Stay there," he said. "Don't turn round."

In cowardice and deep thankfulness, she did as she was told.

Behind her he said, "Can I look closer at the ring, please?"

There was a moment of silence except for the sound of some slight movement. Then Paul said, "It's very strange, but I believe I've seen it before. The other thing—you can wrap it up again, Sergeant. No one's going to be able to identify that for you."

"I brought it because of the ring," the sergeant said. "It was because of the ring the diver saw it. He saw the shine of the silver in the water. And of course the silver fingernails."

Helena gripped the rail in front of her. Leaning forward, she fought to keep the waterfall in focus, but it blurred to a misty gleam.

"I mustn't faint," she thought. "I knew it was something like that. It had to be. And one has to face these things. One can't always be protected. . ."

Paul came to her side. He put a hand on her shoulder and held it with a strong, steadying grip.

"Will you look at this?" he said. "Don't worry, it's nothing hideous. It's just—very strange."

She looked round at what he held.

It was a jade ring, set in silver. It was an unusually large piece of jade, smooth and polished, and would look very beautiful on a long slim hand with silver fingernails. . . .

"*Cleo's!*" she said.

Paul did not answer. He seemed to be searching her face for something, perhaps for doubt, though there was no doubt, or incredulity, on his own. And at once Helena began to doubt, to shrink from certainty. At the same time she felt a prickling in her eyes, as if tears were coming.

"It *can't* be Cleo's," she said. "Can it?"

In a quiet, empty tone, he said, "Yes, it's hers."

"But there must be others just like it," she said. "That woman, the one with Jean——"

"She was Cleo," he said. "I've been half-expecting it

ever since you said perhaps the kidnapper was someone who couldn't drive, Cleo can't drive. And I gave her this ring. There's a date inside it. Just a date—her birthday. I wanted to put something more, but I—I didn't know what. I never know anything like that. So I just had them put the date there." He began to shiver. It was strange, his whole body trembled, yet his voice stayed level. "And now she's in the belly of a crocodile, all but one of her hands, her lovely hands. . . ."

Helena put her arms round him and held him tightly. He leant on her heavily, shaking helplessly. It was the voice of the sergeant that steadied him.

"Then you are able to identify this ring, Dr. Forrest," he said.

Paul drew away from Helena. "Yes."

"And you too, Miss Sebright?"

"I think so," she said.

The sergeant held out his hand and Paul gave the ring back to him.

"It will of course be necessary to show this to the passengers on the Happytime bus," the sergeant went on. "It is possible it has no connection with the woman who is missing from the bus."

"Hardly possible," Paul said.

"Unlikely, perhaps. But anything that is possible must be investigated. If a passenger on the bus noticed this ring on the hand of the woman who is missing, then we are sure she is the person you say."

"And the child?" Helena screwed up her courage to ask.

"Oh, the diving goes on," the sergeant said. "But I don't think we find anything now. I think it is all over with her."

His voice was not at all unkind. It was merely impersonal, businesslike, the voice of a man doing a job to which he was all too accustomed. And after all, in a country where many children died very young of frightening diseases, of malnutrition and through sheer ignorance, why should the death of one more stray child in a river be allowed to disturb the emotions?

Helena and Paul each reached out a hand to the other,

and hand in hand and silent, finished the journey back to the wharf.

They found Mr. Forrest standing in the shade of the sausage tree.

"I got restless," he said. "I wished I'd gone with you. I've telephoned Judy and she wants us to come home. She's adopting the line now that the child on the bus can't have been Jean. I tried to explain there was a good deal of evidence . . ." He stopped as if he had just realised that he was talking on foolishly when the others had something important to say to him. "What's happened, Paul?"

Paul had command of himself now.

"They've found something down in the river," he said. "A hand."

Mr. Forrest straightened his sagging shoulders and looked at the sergeant and the bundle that he was carrying.

"With a ring on it," Paul went on. "And both Helena and I know the ring. It's a jade ring I gave to Cleo Grant for the birthday she had when she was living with us."

The two of them looked at one another.

"Cleo," the old man said softly. "It's difficult to believe, Paul."

"Very difficult," Paul agreed woodenly.

The sergeant said, "If you will all come to the hotel, please, I shall take a statement in writing. And as I have said, I must question the members of the Happytime tour to discover if they saw the woman in their bus wearing this ring. They are on a trip up the river now but will soon return. And I must communicate with my superiors."

"And Jean?" Mr. Forrest asked.

Paul answered, "The diving's going on. The sergeant doesn't think they'll find anything now. But don't forget there's still the car to look for, and the man in the car, with the boot that the tse-tse people probably didn't look into."

"Is that supposed to be comfort?" his father asked.

"It could just be that Jean's still alive, and I prefer that to the thought that she went over the edge with Cleo."

"Cleo," Mr. Forrest murmured. "Poor little Cleo Grant. She could do that to us. Why, Paul?"

"For ransom. For money," Paul replied.

"*Money?*" his father said, almost as if it were something of which he had never heard.

"For Petrzelka."

His father started, perhaps at the cold hatred in Paul's voice. A muscle was throbbing under one of Paul's eyes.

"After all this time?" his father said uncertainly.

"It's the only explanation."

"Was he the man in the car, then? If so, he murdered her, didn't he? He kidnapped Jean and pushed Cleo over the edge."

"He did that to her long ago."

Mr. Forrest looked thoughtfully into his son's face, then took his arm and they started walking to the hotel.

They went into an office that the manager had put at the disposal of the police. The sergeant sat at the manager's desk and wrote laboriously and very slowly, so that his interrogation took a very long time. He asked them about the events of the day before, and again to identify the ring, and about Cleo Grant. Who was she? What was her relationship with them, good or bad?

Good, both the Forrests said. Once, at least. It had once been very good. They had always been very fond of her and had believed that she was fond of them.

And when had they seen her last?

Mr. Forrest said that he had not seen her since the time when she had lived with him and his wife after the death of her parents. Paul had not seen her since he had last been in England, about four years before. Helena had seen her a fortnight ago.

"Just a few days before I came to Uyowa, as a matter of fact," she said. "She helped me to choose some clothes to bring away with me."

"Did she say nothing then of coming to Uyowa?" the sergeant asked.

"Not a word," Helena said. "If she had—well, I suppose

I shouldn't have come, because she'd have been able to bring Jean out here herself."

"But this ring——" It lay on the desk near the sergeant's hand. "You know it?"

"I think so."

"I *know* it's the ring, Sergeant," Paul said. "I've told you why."

"Yes, yes. Exactly. I understand."

Helena felt that it was the one point in the story that the man did understand, though he was working very hard at grasping the rest of it.

"So she comes," he went on, "she is your friend, she steals the child, she brings her here, she throws herself and the child in the river—this story is nonsense. But perhaps it is not nonsense if it is not true that she has a good relationship with you. Perhaps she has a great hatred for you and is taking revenge on you with the child. What do you think?"

Mr. Forrest answered, "Poor Cleo, I don't think she had any hatred for anybody. It was her great failing. She had no discrimination and liked almost everybody far more than they deserved, which is possibly a way of saying that she didn't like anyone enough to be capable of hatred."

It completely confused the sergeant. He looked up with some relief as the door opened and one of his men came in and spoke to him rapidly in his own language.

He interpreted, "The launch with the Happytime people has returned. Now we will ask them if they saw the ring on the missing woman. Please wait here."

He went out, taking the ring with him.

"A sensible man," Mr. Forrest observed as the door closed. "Well educated. We're fortunate. Things could have been worse."

In a few minutes the sergeant returned and sat down at the desk again.

"The American lady and the French gentleman have both identified the ring," he said. "They saw it on the hand of the woman in the bus. They are sure of this. They say also she had silver fingernails. All this will be reported to Tondolo. The police there will discover when this woman, Miss Grant, entered the country, and no doubt how and why she took the child away with her. If you wish to return now to Tondolo you may do so, Mr. Forrest. I advise you to go. There is nothing you can do here. But you may also wait here if you prefer. I must return to the river now, but I tell you my honest opinion is nothing more will be found. We know this river very well here. What you do not find at once you never find at all. I am very sorry."

"I think, all the same, we'll wait for a time," Mr. Forrest said.

"Just as you like. I go now," the sergeant said, and pocketing the ring, went out again.

The Forrests and Helena waited until the middle of the afternoon. They were told then that the diving had been given up. At last Mr. Forrest dispatched a long cable to Denis. After that he telephoned his wife again to tell her what had happened and that the three of them were returning home. Silently, they went to their rooms, fetched their few belongings and started the long drive back to Tondolo.

It did not take nearly as long as the drive out had taken. There were no soldiers about to stop them and they had no puncture or other mishap. Yet to Helena the journey seemed far longer than that of the day before, although she was almost unconscious of the jolting and the dust, of the countryside with its banana plantations, its round thatched huts, its flaming erythrinas, and the flying stones of which the roadside notices told them to be aware. Indeed, it was this very emptiness of her mind that made time seem endless. She did not notice the short dusk deepen into darkness, only, after a time, she realised that in fact darkness had come, unbroken on all sides, except by the long shaft of their own headlights.

When she thought at all it was mostly of Cleo. Not of Jean, that was too painful. She thought of Cleo and Paul, of how he had suspected Cleo of being the kidnapper long before she had. That disconnected sentence of his yesterday, as he and Helena had sat by the waterfall, how

had it gone? It had been something about a private nightmare
that had been growing on him, about Josiah lying to
his father in the morning, about the missing spare wheel,
about a kidnapping by bus, and about how it all added
up. . . . Added up because Cleo, who couldn't drive, would
have had to take Jean by bus to the rendezvous with
Petrzelka. Added up because Josiah, who had been with
the Forrests for years, had known Cleo and perhaps would
have lied, punctured the tyre and removed the spare wheel
for her. Added up because Paul had known Cleo too
and what she was capable of with a clear-eyed lack of
illusion, even though he had certainly been far more in
love with her once than he now admitted. And had
never quite got over it, any more than Cleo had got over
Petrzelka. And perhaps never would. Helena's heart raced
suddenly with a new and startling fear. She had not understood till that moment how much that could matter.

It was nearly ten o'clock when the car reached the first
lit-up streets of Tondolo. Lit-up but empty and silent, as
the town seemed always to become quite early in the evening.
Paul turned the car into the road up the hill to the Forrests'
house. The street-lamps shone on bougainvillaea, cassia,
jacaranda, in the gardens lining the road. There were lights
here in the houses and on the comfortable verandahs where
people sat with their drinks, their friends, their transistors,
enjoying what they probably found the pleasantest part of
the day.

There were lights in the Forrests' house. At a first glance
from the road, Helena thought that every light in the house
must have been turned on, then she realised that the garden
was full of lights too, lights which moved, shining momentarily on one dark figure, then shifting to pick up another.
The garden was full of people as well as of lights.

"What the devil——?" Paul began as he pulled on the
wheel to turn the car in at the gate.

The car gave a soft, sickening jolt.

He stopped it with a fierce jerk, and jumping out, stooped
quickly to look at what lay in the road between the wheels,

then slowly straightened up again with a look of shock and disgust on his face.

Helena got out of the car too and stood beside him.

It was the dead body of Bongo that lay in the road. But it was not the car that had killed the puppy. He had been strangled by a cord pulled tight round his throat. A street lamp overhead lit up the dull gleam of the pennies that had been scattered over him.

CHAPTER IX

Paul stooped again and picked up the dead puppy.

He was turning towards the gate when Mr. Forrest said, "Give him to me. You take the car in."

He took the puppy from Paul, and holding it in his arms, walked in at the gate. Helena followed him. Paul got back into the car and drove it slowly after them.

Several dark figures converged on them in the garden, yet did not come close or speak to them. It seemed to Helena that there was a furtive sort of apprehensiveness in the bright eyes that glinted around them in the shifting lights of the electric torches. Imagination? Probably. It was hardly possible that a group of policemen, for that was what they were, could be frightened of the corpse of a puppy, put out in the road with pennies scattered over him to save some unfortunate from the effects of a spell. Yet she herself was scared, and not only by the unexplained presence of the men. She felt the uncleanness of magic, the malice in it, clinging to the limp body of poor Bongo.

Someone came towards them from the house, walking deliberately, a short, rather plump, middle-aged man, dressed in a neat, dark suit, a white shirt and dark tie.

Mr. Forrest greeted him. "Good evening, Superintendent. I suppose you can explain this intrusion."

"Good evening, Mr. Forrest," the short man said. "I am very sorry for it."

His English was almost perfect, except for the way that he spat out his consonants, which gave his quiet speech a sound of excitability oddly in contrast to the stolidity of his round, dark face.

"My wife——?" Mr. Forrest said quickly.

"In the house. No need to worry yourself about her. If you will come in I will explain what has happened."

"Is it something to do with my granddaughter?"

"No. I am sorry, no. This is quite another matter."

"But you know of her disappearance?"

"Yes, yes. The police at Ross Falls have of course been in communication with us. I am very sorry for you. I offer you my sincere condolences. But this is another matter. If you will please come in. . . ."

"I think I'll bury this dog first." Mr. Forrest looked at where his pergola had stood, where two men were now digging in the loose soil that surrounded the stumps of the pillars. "If I could have one of those spades for a few minutes, Mr. Ngau . . ."

"I'll do it," Paul said.

Superintendent Ngau nodded and gave an order. One of the diggers came forward and gave Paul his spade. Paul took the dead Bongo from his father and walked away across the lawn to a flowerbed and started digging.

Mr. Forrest said, "I suppose you don't know who did that—killed the dog, I mean?"

"I am afraid I have not inquired into it, having other more urgent matters to consider," Superintendent Ngau replied. "I would guess, however, it was probably your servant Josiah. He is of the old school, ignorant and superstitious."

"I can't imagine it," Mr. Forrest said. "He's a kind soul—we've known him for years—and he was quite fond of the dog."

"That would not come into it. He would be thinking of helping this household by exorcising the evil that has come to it. And he would not in any case have your British feeling for animals. You know all that very well, Mr. Forrest."

"Yes, I suppose I do. All the same . . . But let's go in."

He led the way into the house.

Mrs. Forrest, who was in the sitting-room, rose quickly from her chair when her husband came in and held him tightly in her arms. She was in her black slacks and brightly patterned shirt. Its colours took the last vestiges of colour from her face. Her eyes were unnaturally staring.

"You've heard nothing about Jean?" she asked.

He shook his head.

E

"And Cleo?"

"Just what I told you on the telephone."

"Cleo!" she said. "That she could do it! To us!" She looked round. "Where's Paul?"

"Burying Bongo in the garden. Did you know Bongo had been killed?"

"No. Poor Bongo. He's been maddening all day, barking at every sound. You could tell he knew something was wrong. How was he killed? Was he run over?"

"No. We'll talk about it later. Now, Superintendent, I'd be glad to hear what your men are doing digging up my garden."

Before the policemen could answer, Mrs. Forrest cried out, "It's insufferable, Hugh! I can't tell you how fearful it's been—how furious I am! They came here an hour ago, they arrested all the servants, they went through the house, they started to dig. I told them they'd no right to do any of it. I telephoned Robbie Meldrum, but he was still away, doing something about those awful murders somewhere. I was all alone, except that Peg Passfield dropped in, I suppose meaning to be kind, though it was almost the last straw, having to listen to how all her servants had gone too and without even being arrested. Well, I did what I could here this evening, I said that everything these men were doing was outrageous, but they wouldn't listen to me and in the end I couldn't do anything. I've just sat here and waited for you to come back. Perhaps you can do something."

Superintendent Ngau came forward from behind Helena. In the light of the room his eyes had a yellow gleam. Their pupils were light brown, the whites almost amber.

"Mrs. Forrest, I have told you how sorry I am to be compelled to do this at such a time," he said. "But it is quite unavoidable. It is my duty. On information received from the man Wilbraham Ngugi, I am compelled to make this search and to arrest your servants. When they have been interrogated it may be they will be released again. I do not promise this. In my belief they are all guilty together. But I promise you they will all be treated with the utmost fairness."

"Fairness!" she cried. "Were you fair to Wilbraham? What did you do to him? Beat him till he confessed all you wanted—then shot him? Is that what you've done?"

"Mrs. Forrest, Mrs. Forrest," he said. "He confessed, yes, that he had been involved in the attempt on the life of President Mukasa. But I do not know why you should make these allegations of brutality against us. The man is a criminal who has made a free statement that he took part in an attempted murder."

"As Josiah and Erasmus and Malcolm and Joe and Horace are all going to make free statements now, with guns pushed into the backs of their necks!"

"Judy, please." Her husband pressed her back into her chair. "Do give me a chance to find out what's happened. Sit down, Superintendent. You too, Helena, you look quite exhausted. I think we all need a drink." He raised his voice, "Joe——! No, of course, how stupid of me, he isn't there, is he? Well, wait a moment, I'll get them." He disappeared into the dining-room, coming back after a minute or two with a tray of glasses, a bottle of whisky and a siphon. "You'll join us, won't you, Superintendent?"

"Thank you," Mr. Ngau said, and Mr. Forrest poured out five stiff drinks.

Paul came in, earth on his hands, as he was doing it. He went straight out to wash his hands, then, on returning, sat down on the arm of his mother's chair and put an arm round her shoulders.

"Well now," Mr. Forrest said.

"As I have just told you," the superintendent replied, "the man, Wilbraham Ngugi, has confessed to having taken part in an attempt on the life of President Mukasa, by having been one of a party that threw a grenade at the car of the president when he was on his way home from a reception at the new Institute of Technology. It was only by a miracle that the president escaped. It was the car behind him that received the force of the explosion. One man was killed and two were badly injured. One of them may die."

"And Wilbraham is dead?" Mr. Forrest asked.

Superintendent Ngau looked down at the pointed toes of his highly polished shoes.

"It was not only murder, it was treason," he murmured.

"But without a trial?"

"You will no doubt be officially notified of his fate in due course. I have no official information myself."

Mrs. Forrest gave a snort of violent contempt. "No one ever has official information about anything nowadays. Everyone lies, evades, dodges. It's all fear and corruption. And here's my granddaughter been kidnapped, probably dead, and you do nothing, nothing!"

Helena saw Paul press on his mother's shoulder to quiet her.

"Why are you digging up the garden, Superintendent?" he asked. "What are you looking for?"

"Ngugi confessed that there were more arms hidden here." The superintendent held his tumbler up to the light and gazed at it. Its colour almost matched his curious eyes. "Among the pillars, he told us."

"My poor swaying pillars," Mr. Forrest said. "So that's why they kept falling down. I suppose he couldn't afford to let me get the ground raked over and planted up while he still needed to get hold of those arms. And I thought it was because I hadn't learnt enough about building, hadn't troubled enough with the foundations. And perhaps it's true in a sense that I hadn't. What do you think, Superintendent? We came along, we British, with unpractical ideas of building a society on all sorts of unsteady pillars—parliamentary government, justice, law and order—but we left the foundations to look after themselves. A waste of everyone's time, really."

The superintendent gave a little hissing laugh. "Yes, yes, no doubt." He laughed softly again. It sounded as if he were whispering "tsi-tsi, tsi-tsi," to himself. "No doubt, no doubt."

Paul asked, "Did Wilbraham actually implicate any of the other servants?"

"He implicated a number of people before he finished. Apart from that, we have our own suspicions. Now I will go

out and see how the digging is proceeding." Mr. Ngau
finished his drink and stood up. "You will all stay here
please for the present. I have no wish to inconvenience you
or distress you unnecessarily at a time when you are so
concerned about the fate of your granddaughter, but I shall
have other questions I must put to you presently. Thank
you."

He went out into the garden.

Mrs. Forrest caught her husband's hand. "Hugh, Denis
will be ringing up soon, won't he? Any time now. How
can we speak to him? What can we say?"

"I'll do it," Paul said. "I'm hardened."

He walked out on to the verandah and stood looking after
Mr. Ngau.

She went on, "It seems almost funny now, but d'you
know what I did the day before yesterday? When we
were at the Passfields', I asked Vernon Elder if he would
offer Helena a job. I thought if we could persuade her to
stay on—since it was obvious, you see, that there wasn't
any important relationship between her and Denis, as we
thought when we heard she was coming,—I thought, if she'd
stay, we could find reasons for keeping Jean here till Denis
came to fetch her. And once he came, I was sure we could
keep him. And now he *will* be coming, and Marcia too, but
Jean—oh God, Hugh, I feel wicked even to have thought
of it!"

"Here they come—they've found something," Paul said,
and a moment afterwards several men appeared on the
verandah, two of them carrying an oblong box, with the
red soil of the garden sticking to it, and two more carrying
a small, square chest.

Superintendent Ngau followed them.

"Put these things down here," he said, and as they obeyed
him, went into the sitting-room.

"Rifles and grenades," Mr. Forrest," he said. "Would
you like to come and look at them?"

Paul was already looking at them. Mr. and Mrs. Forrest
and Helena went out on to the verandah together and
looked into the boxes. Helena knew nothing about firearms,

but to her the rifles looked new and clean and deadly, while the grenades looked rather like some odd sort of harmless toy. She thought of Wilbraham with his gleaming, genial smile, of amiable, giggling Horace, of clever, moody Joe, and of gentle, abstracted old Josiah, and wondered how this group of men had ever managed to get themselves involved with these modern tools of destruction. As they evidently had. No one seemed to think that there was any point in arguing about that.

"Well, what next?" Mr. Forrest asked, meeting the amber eyes of the superintendent.

"My men must dig further, in case there are more," he replied. "I think these are all, but it is necessary to be sure. Meanwhile it will be best, I think, if you all come down to the police station with me to make statements of what you know." There had been a slight change in his manner. His voice had a new ring in it and his eyes seemed brighter. "I hope you will not argue about this. I should not like to have to compel such an eminent citizen of Tondolo as Mr. Forrest, one to whom we all owe so much, to accompany me. It would be better to keep it on a friendly basis. Entirely friendly. I am sure you will agree."

"You know, of course, that none of us knows anything," Mr. Forrest said.

The superintendent shrugged his shoulders. "Many of us do not know what we know."

"It's intolerable!" Mrs. Forrest cried violently. "Intolerable. I won't go." She sat down abruptly on one of the verandah chairs and folded her hands in her lap. "You may ask me any questions you like here, Superintendent, and I will do my best to answer them, but I'm not going down to that place of yours in the town, along with the drunks you've scraped off the pavement and the beggars and the petty thieves—not for anything you can say."

"I think it will be better if you come, Mrs. Forrest," he said. "I am sorry to have to remind you of it, but only two days ago you were heard to say to a large gathering of people that it was a pity the plot against the life of President Mukasa had not been successful. I shall want to ask you a few questions concerning that and your opinions in general."

"I said *what*?" Mrs. Forrest exclaimed. "Oh, I remember——!"

"Mother!" Paul said warningly.

"But it wasn't serious," she said. "It was just the sort of thing one says at a party. No, I'm not going. For one thing, and it's very important, much more important than this ridiculous charge against us—we're expecting a telephone call from Denis. My son Denis, Superintendent, the father of the child who's disappeared. He's in the United States and we sent him a cable earlier to-day. He's certain to telephone soon and we must be here to answer him."

"I know of your son Denis," the policeman said. "He is a friend of Gilbert Kaggwa. I believe they were students together at Oxford. But it is not a good thing now to be a friend of Kaggwa, a traitor and a murderer. Apart from that, you have not been charged with anything. You are only being asked to help us in our inquiries."

"Then do your inquiring here."

"Just a minute, Judy," Mr. Forrest said. "Superintendent, we'll come to the police station with you if you wish it, but what my wife said is true, we're expecting a call from my son sometime this evening, and it would be the grossest inhumanity to leave no one here to answer it. I'm sure you'll agree with me on that. So suppose only my wife and I go with you and you leave Miss Sebright and my son Paul here. Miss Sebright, after all, is only a visitor to Uyowa. She actually arrived in Tondolo some days after the attack on Mr. Mukasa. So you can't suspect her of anything in connection with it, or of having any knowledge that could be useful to you."

"Yes, that is true," Mr. Ngau agreed. "She shall then, if she wishes, remain here. But it would be better for Dr. Forrest to accompany us. He has been seen digging round the pillars with you in your garden and it is surprising that he should have noticed nothing unusual in the ground there. He will be asked to account for it."

"Well, Helena, do you mind being left here alone to wait for that call from Denis?" Mr. Forrest asked.

"She will not be alone," the superintendent said. "I shall leave guards in the garden. And it is to be understood that she is not to leave the house."

"Thank you," Mr. Forrest said. "Helena, do you mind staying here?"

"Of course not," she said, only realising as she did so that once they were all gone she was probably going to mind it very much indeed.

Perhaps it showed in her face, for Paul touched her hand and said, "Don't worry, we'll soon be back."

"Of course, of course," Superintendent Ngau said and gave his little hissing laugh, "Tsi-tsi, tsi-tsi."

It left Helena wondering when the Forrests in fact would be back, and thinking that perhaps it would not be soon.

"Lock up behind us," Mr. Forrest said to her.

"And don't open to anyone you don't know," Mrs. Forrest added.

"There will be no one," the superintendent said. "No one will be permitted to enter."

He stood aside to shepherd the three Forrests out ahead of him.

When they had gone Helena not only locked and bolted the doors, taking special care with the glass doors on to the verandah, but because she felt troubled by the blank, dark stare of the windows, covered by their wire screens, she drew all the curtains of the ground floor rooms.

Then she began to think that that had been a mistake. By muffling all the noises of the outside world, the faint music of a radio in a nearby house, the occasional sound of a passing car, the things that reminded her of normal lives going on around her, it sharply increased her sense of solitude and made the silence in the house weigh more heavily on her nerves. She didn't usually mind solitude. In London the moment when she closed the door of her flat behind her, and saw its economically acquired but genuine and dear comforts waiting for her, was one of the best of the day.

Only a very bad mood could spoil it, a mood when the little flat seemed to her simply an empty, lonely and unwelcoming place, from which she must rush out at once to find friends, go to a cinema, eat out, do anything, a mood such as the one that had sent her out into the damp cold of a January evening, by chance to meet Cleo Grant.

Helena shrank from the thought. But she shrank from almost every other thought that came into her mind. Jean. Ross Falls. Crocodiles. Paul and Cleo. And the telephone call that was coming. Paul had said that he was hardened to breaking bad news, but Helena was not. Had she ever had to do it? No, not serious bad news. Her life had been very, very sheltered. And she had never even noticed it.

What would she say to that voice from across half the world?

Better not to plan, she thought. If she tried to decide in advance what to say, she was certain to say something quite different. Better to keep her mind as blank as possible. Sit it out. Wait.

With the curtains drawn the room was beginning to feel insufferably hot. She went to a window and grasped a curtain to pull it back. Then she thought of the guards in the garden, silent now, who, if she did draw the curtains back, would be able to watch every movement that she made. She let the curtain go again. But as she roamed about the room, she wondered how she could possibly get through the evening ahead, and perhaps more than the evening, perhaps the whole night.

Suddenly she was aware of intense hunger, nervous hunger, sharp and painful. She went into the kitchen, found bread and cheese and instant coffee, made a cup of coffee and a sandwich and took them back to the sitting-room. All the time the centre of her attention was the telephone. It was on a small carved table in a corner of the room. Olive wood was what the table was made of, she believed, and it had been carved locally. She had seen others just like it in the shops in Tondolo. It was a pleasant creamy colour, with a faint greenish tinge. And the telephone was black, shiny black and uncompromising. Not a friendly telephone, not a kind one, linking her to friends. But hypnotic, keeping her staring at it, all her muscles tense, so that she could leap at it the moment the bell started to ring.

The telephone's hypnotic hold on her probably helped her to drift presently into a half-sleep as she sat in one of the chairs, and when at last it did begin to ring she did not answer it at once, because she thought that it was her alarm clock on her bedside table in her flat in London, and only put out a fumbling hand to turn it off.

Her hand found and knocked over a vase of canna lilies. The crash and the splash of water over her feet shocked the drowsiness out of her. She sprang up and snatched up the telephone and gabbled into it the number that she read on the dial.

There was a short silence, then a man's voice said, "Mrs. Forrest?"

The operator, she supposed. The voice had a strong foreign accent. He pronounced the rs in Forrest with a heavy guttural roll.

"No, she's not here, but I can take the call," Helena said.

"Mrs. Forrest," the voice repeated. "I want to speak to Mrs. Forrest."

"She's not here."

"Then Mr. Forrest, please."

"He isn't here either. But I told you, I can take the call."

"Who are you?"

"I'm Miss Sebright. Helena Sebright. A friend of theirs."

"Ah. I will call again then."

"Wait!" She had realised that this was not the accent of any African telephone operator, trying to connect her with America. The foreignness of the accent was certainly European. "Who are you? What do you want?"

"No need to say. I can ring later."

Her heart began to beat painfully. "Can't you leave a message?"

"A message? Very well. You may say the child is safe and will remain so if my instructions are carefully followed."

"What instructions?"

"None now, except to say you would be very unwise to communicate with the police. Good-bye."

"Wait!" she begged again. "You say Jean's safe. She's alive?"

"She is alive."

"How do I know you're speaking the truth?"

The voice answered, " 'What is truth? said jesting Pilate.' Ha, ha! Good joke."

The line went dead.

Helena went on talking frantically into the telephone for a moment, imploring it to tell her more. Then, shakily, she put it down, and it was only then that she saw that she was not alone in the room. A small, slightly built African in the usual long white garment had come soundlessly in, she did not know from where. For an instant she thought that he was one of the servants who after all had been left behind, then she realised that he was someone whom she had never seen before.

At the look of fear on her face he raised a slender hand and cafe a step farther into the room.

"I am very sorry if I startled you," he said. "Please do not be afraid of me. I am a very harmless and helpless man. I am Gilbert Kaggwa."

CHAPTER X

Helena's first instinctive action was to look at all the windows.

He said with a smile, "Oh, if I hadn't been sure the curtains were drawn I shouldn't have appeared. As it is, I think we're quite safe for the moment."

He had a deep, soft voice and his English was faultless. "How did you get in?"

Helena's hand had tightened on the telephone. But that was from shock. The shock of the kidnapper's call and of this man's sudden appearance. She had no intention of calling anyone. Who was there for her to call?

"I've been in for some time," he replied. "For the last forty-eight hours, to be exact."

"Forty-eight hours—two days—in this house?"

"In the servants' quarters until the police arrived here this evening, when I hid in the roof."

"And the Forrests knew you were here all the time! They've had that to add to all their other troubles."

"Please." He was shorter than Helena, and he stooped slightly. He had delicate bones and finely modelled features. With the gleam of his bright, wary eyes, it gave him a rather birdlike look. "Do you think we might sit down and talk for a little? There's a favour I want to ask you."

She sat down abruptly in the nearest chair. He sat down facing her.

"The Forrests didn't know I was here," he said. "They knew nothing about it. They still know nothing about it. So I hope they'll be back just as soon as our friend Ngau has shown how tough he can be with influential white people. He doesn't really believe that Mr. Forrest had any suspicion of those arms being hidden in the patch of ground where he was trying to erect his poor pergola, or that Mrs. Forrest meant what she said about Mr. Mukasa. She may slightly prefer me to Mukasa, but not to the extent of abetting any plot against him. And Ngau himself has no suspicion of my being here. If he'd ever thought of such a thing, he'd have searched the house from top to bottom, instead of taking only a casual look round. He came to search the garden for arms. He wasn't looking for me."

"But the servants knew you were here," she said.

"Ah yes, naturally."

"Well, suppose they talk now."

He gave a shrug of his narrow shoulders. "I don't think they'll falsely incriminate the Forrests. Why should they want to? We like to think we manage our own affairs now, you know, even our revolutions. We don't need help from the British."

"Even your murders, don't you mean?" she said. "To me a revolution just means killing—lots of unnecessary killing, mostly of people who don't care one way or the other about the issues you want them to fight about."

"Miss Sebright, you've lived all your life in the most stable country in the world—do you think you really know what you're talking about?" He gave a pleasant smile.

Helena found that she could not help responding to it. She was not sure that she wanted to like him, but she was already beginning to do so. "Of course I could hardly know less, Mr. Kaggwa."

"I promise you I don't want any killing that can be avoided," he said. "But some weeks ago some of my friends were killed—butchered most horribly, some with their wives and children,—all to put this man Mukasa in power. And not even for what he is himself, but simply because he's too weak not to do what a group of ambitious army officers tell him. And all they want is to plunder the people and enrich themselves. Is this to succeed? Is no one to raise a hand against it?"

"But can you be any use now? Isn't it too late?"

"Because those arms were discovered? My dear Miss Sebright, those are not all we have. And these men who were arrested here to-day are not my only supporters."

"Those poor men. It's thinking of them just now that makes it all so hateful," she said, "whatever the rights and wrongs are. Simple, ignorant men like that. They're the ones who'll pay, without having the faintest idea what they're paying for."

"My friends paid, Miss Sebright—not simple or ignorant men. And I shouldn't say my own life-expectancy is very great at the moment. Particularly as I'm beginning to doubt if you'll be as willing to help me as I hoped you would."

"Oh, I'll help, if I can," she said. "The Forrests would help you, wouldn't they? They think a lot of you. I owe it to them."

"Ah, the Forrests," he said. "I've been wishing with all my heart I'd never come here, considering what it's brought on them."

"But you just said the police have no suspicion you're here," she said. "You said the Forrests aren't in any serious trouble."

"Ah yes, that's correct. Not with the police. No, I was thinking of the child."

She came up out of her ·ir. "The child—Jean? You'd something to do with that? ᵦf you had, I won't do anything to help you' I'll start screaming till those guards outside come in!"

"No, no, please," he said urgently, "wait a minute. Listen to me. It wasn't as you mean. I had certain knowledge, that's all, and I didn't understand its import till the servants told me about the tragedy at Ross Falls. They only knew of it themselves when Mr. Forrest telephoned his wife this afternoon. But if I'd understood in time I could probably have prevented it."

"Go on," Helena said. "Tell me what happened."

"Sit down, please," he said. "Do please sit down. I am very tired. You don't know how tired I am. So I find it much easier to talk sitting down than standing up. And it's always easier to talk reasonably sitting than standing, haven't you noticed that? Tempers don't flare so easily. I think perhaps that's why the politicians of the world keep talking about getting us all to sit round a table. That wonderful Table that's going to solve all our difficulties. I'm not sure that in our era it hasn't become a more potent symbol than the Cross."

Helena sat down again, but only on the edge of her chair. "Tell me what happened."

"Well, as you can guess," he said, "for the last few weeks I've been moving from one hiding place to another. It would have been easier to get right away, but it was necessary for me to stay in the district to direct the attempts of my supporters to overthrow the present régime; also to take charge immediately if we were successful. This is not simply personal ambition. The truth is that I'm more likely than anyone else to be able to prevent the excesses that follow a coup."

"About Jean," Helena said. "That's what I want to know. Can't we skip the politics?"

"I'm afraid I have to explain a little," he said. "There've been two such attempted coups, as you probably know. One was to have begun with the ambush of Mukasa and his associates on their return from the reception held at the new Institute of Technology. It was unsuccessful. The second began in the barracks a few days ago. You probably heard the shooting. It was unsuccessful too."

"Perhaps you aren't too good at directing that sort of thing," Helena said.

He spread his hands with their pink palms upward. "I'm sure I'm not very good at directing violence, Miss Sebright. One is good at the things one enjoys. However, after these two failures, we intended to try at least once more. But the time had come when I had to change my hiding place yet again, and then, the day before yesterday, very hurriedly again, because the police, who are fairly certain that I'm in Tondolo, had become suspicious of the people who'd taken me in. And there was very little time to make new arrangements. So Joe, one of the house-boys here, a very able, reliable man, suggested that I should stay here in the servants' quarters till this evening. He said that all the family except the child were going out to a party, and the child would be in bed. I could come in without their knowledge and leave again sometime in the darkness without any of them ever knowing that I'd been here." He gave a briefly regretful sigh, as if he knew that it would have been best for all if he had said no then, had not listened to Joe, the able and reliable. "I didn't like the plan. The Forrests are my friends and I didn't want to involve them in any danger on my account. But I didn't know what else to do. And all would have been well if it hadn't happened that, just as I came up to the house, I came face to face with Miss Grant."

"You knew her, then," Helena said.

"Oh yes, I was often a guest in this house when she was living here. I remembered her very well, a tragic, winning, but unbalanced girl. I felt very sorry for her at the time, yet there was always something about her that I distrusted, a weakness of character, you know. She took her troubles too hard. She went under to them too completely. However, that isn't the point. The fact is, when we met here it was just when neither of us could afford to let anyone else know of our having been here at all."

"I see. I think I see. Only I'm not sure I do." Helena rested her head in her hands. "How did Cleo get into the house? And why? Why didn't any of you do anything to stop her?"

"She got in because Josiah let her in," Gilbert Kaggwa said. "He was working here already when she stayed with the Forrests, he remembered her and he saw nothing strange or wrong in her sudden arrival. He let her go upstairs and talk to the child without any misgivings. And perhaps some money passed to ensure his silence, and that of the other servants, about her visit. I think she told them she wanted to give the Forrests a surprise next day, or something like that."

"So when you met her, you were both awfully ready to agree that neither of you should say anything to the Forrests about the other."

"Exactly."

"And you'd no suspicions? You aren't like old Josiah. Didn't you think there was anything strange about this secrecy of hers?"

He took a moment to answer, then said reluctantly, "Yes, I thought it was strange. But Miss Grant had always been strange. I imagined, I suppose, that she'd some odd sentimental reason for coming to the house in this way. Obviously she'd waited for a time when all the family was out. But certainly I suspected no evil and I was very thankful when she suggested that we should simply say nothing to anyone of having met here. I didn't even know of the presence of the child. I didn't know that the child had followed Miss Grant downstairs and had actually seen me come in. It was only later in the evening that Joe told me about that, and when I asked if she wasn't likely to betray me, he told me there was no reason to worry, because she was leaving early in the morning with Miss Grant for a trip to Ross Falls and by the time she returned I'd be gone."

"And it didn't strike you there was anything queer about Jean's going off on a trip like that without the Forrests knowing?"

"I'm afraid that's where my grave responsibility arises, Miss Sebright," Gilbert Kaggwa answered. "If I'd put together this trip to the Game Park with Miss Grant's desire for secrecy, I should not have been able to overlook the fact that there was something very wrong in the situation. But a hunted man is selfish. I didn't think. As long as there was no risk of the child betraying me, I didn't want to think about her. I was very much occupied with my own predicament and very tired."

"I suppose it was Erasmus who arranged that slow puncture and removed the spare wheel from the car," Helena said.

"Yes, because, through the note no one had guessed the child would leave behind, you'd got on to her trail far faster than had been anticipated and there appeared to be every likelihood that you'd bring her back before nightfall."

"Who killed Bongo?"

"The dog? That was Joe."

"Why?"

"Because it kept barking, knowing that there was a stranger in the house. The pennies scattered over it were merely a ruse to conceal the real motive for the killing."

"And Josiah didn't like any of it, did he?" Helena said. "He didn't like having to lie to the Forrests."

"No, he was very uneasy at saying nothing. He's worked for different members of Mrs. Forrest's family since his boyhood and he's very attached to them. But with the child having seen me, even he agreed it was best to have her out of the way for a day or two."

"And now that day or two may be for ever!" Helena dropped her head into her hands to avoid the sad, steady gaze of his eyes which caught at her sympathy even when she wanted only to be angry.

"But she's alive—I heard you say on the telephone that she's alive," he said.

"I was talking to her kidnapper," Helena said. "Does a kidnapper ever let his victim get back alive? And how do we know for certain that she is alive? How can one believe anything a—a creature like that says?"

"You mustn't despair. Truly, you should never despair."

Helena did not answer, but after a moment she raised her head and looked at him again.

She still did not want to like him, because of what his coming to this house had caused, yet she could not help responding to the sympathy on his face. She reminded herself that he could not really be quite the kind and gentle man that he looked. He was not averse to having his followers lob grenades at his enemies. Probably he was capable of giving orders to a firing squad and sleeping soundly afterwards. He had blood, if only vicariously, on his slim little hands. And soon he would have more, if he was successful in what he wanted to do. Yet she found that she did like him and was very sorry for him because of the rings of dark shadow round his eyes and the withered look of his lips, the look that comes from pain or extreme exhaustion.

"You said you wanted to ask me a favour," she said. "What is it?"

He wiped a hand over his forehead and it came away wet. Briefly she wondered what might have happened to her if she had not been co-operative.

"I must leave this house," he said. "The sooner the better for the sake of the Forrests, as well as my own."

"But there are guards in the garden."

"Yes, and so their attention must be distracted."

"How? Do you want me to go out and talk to them?"

"Please, I don't want you to attempt anything so dangerous," he said, "or so suspicious, if you don't mind my saying so. But I've a plan—not a very good plan, but the best I can think of—which won't appear to involve you at all. It's that you should telephone some friends of yours and tell them that you've been left here alone because the Forrests have been taken to the police station. Say that you're afraid, and won't they please come and keep you company? I'll be very surprised if no one comes to your help. And you should warn them, on account of the guards in the garden, to sound their horns loudly at the gate before attempting to drive in. Also they should not come in at all without the guards' permission. We don't want casualties."

"The guards won't let them in," Helena said. "They were told not to let anyone in."

"That doesn't matter. The important thing is that I should hear the horn and know when the guards are occupied at the gate. Then I can slip out quietly at the back, climb the fence and get away down the road into the town."

"You've somewhere to go to?"

"I think so."

"You aren't sure?"

"I'm sure I must leave here, Miss Sebright. After that, I must hope for the best."

"There's just one snag about your plan," she said, "and that is that it happens I haven't any friends here."

It took him aback. He looked as if he thought this was some strange and subtle trick that she was trying to play on him. Then his face cleared. "Ah yes, of course, you've only just arrived in Tondolo. But this needn't be a lifelong friend, you know. Anyone will do. Anyone to whom you can say that you're alone here and afraid. Say there are guards in the garden—black guards, dangerous coloured men—and that you're afraid. It will be very surprising if there's no one, in the circumstances, who'll come to the rescue of a white woman."

She gave a hard little laugh. "That's really what you want me to say, Mr. Kaggwa?"

They exchanged a look, then he gave a wry smile. "Miss Sebright, I know you aren't a person who'd say that of your own accord. It's simply that it will work, and that's all that concerns me at the moment."

"All right," she said, "but I still don't know whom to call. I haven't met many people yet. There's Superintendent Meldrum, if he's home now. He's been away all day——"

"Not him," Gilbert Kaggwa said quickly. "Being himself a policeman, the guards would probably let him straight in and we don't want that. What we want is an argument at the gate."

"Well then, there are Mr. and Mrs. Passfield—I've been to their house—and there's Mr. Elder, of the British Council. I believe he's meaning to offer me a job."

"Any of those," he said.

"Then I'll try the Passfields first." She picked up the telephone directory.

As she turned the pages Gilbert Kaggwa got up and started to walk about the room. He walked quite soundlessly. It was only because, as she read, she saw out of the corner of her eye the flicker of his long white garment, that she knew that he was moving about. As soon as she dialled, he froze where he stood.

The shrill voice of Peg Passfield answered.

"Mrs. Passfield?" Helena said. "This is Helena Sebright. D'you remember me? I came to your house yesterday with the Forrests. I——"

"Of course, of course I remember you!" Peg Passfield broke in so stridently that the words carried all over the room. "You're the pretty girl Paul couldn't keep his eyes off. Our celibate Paul, who was never going to notice another woman because his heart had been broken by that Cleo woman. My dear, I never believed all that myself for a moment, but that's the way they all talk out here. Nothing but gossip and scandal. It makes me go screaming mad. I don't mean I'm a partciularly brilliant woman. I don't say my conversation shines. But I do think the way we all just sit around and call each other names is simply the end. Try to do anything, drop a hint, for instance, that you've actually opened a book and looked inside it, I mean, and people look at you as if you've taken leave of your senses."

"Mrs. Passfield," Helena said, "I wonder if I could speak to your husband for a moment."

"Jim?" the telephone screeched back at her. "You want to speak to Jim? Oh, my dear, don't tell me you're another of the poor women he's bowled over with that fatal charm of his! You wouldn't think he had it, would you, just to look at him? I mean, with him starting to get a little pot-belly and all, poor, sweet Jim. But he's got something, or he thinks he has, or else he just thinks I ought to think so, because he keeps telling me all about it. Honestly, I could die laughing sometimes. Masculine vanity! They just won't give up, will they, even with middle-age howling at the door? In fact, they get worse——"

"Please, Mrs. Passfield," Helena said, beginning to feel frantic, "something very important has come up and I've got to get advice from someone. I thought perhaps your husband——"

"Not Jim, darling!" Peg Passfield shouted. "Sorry, but he isn't here. I'm furious with him, because he simply came in and went out again, leaving me all alone. I mean it, absolutely alone, because things came to a head this morning with those awful brutes I had for servants and I simply turned them out. So I'm sitting in this house all by myself and I wouldn't admit it to everyone, but I simply quake with fear at every sound. I'm the most frightful coward! Ha, ha." She gave a gay little scream of laughter to show that of course she had never known fear in her life and, as everyone knew, was really of the stuff that had built an empire. "Not that it isn't a relief to have made up my mind about those creatures. We had simply the most enormous row this morning——"

"Please, could you give me any idea where I could get

in touch with your husband?" Helena said. "Is he at his office?"

"As a matter of fact, I believe he's at the police station," Peg Passfield said. "He got a message——"

"Then he's heard what's happened!" Helena exclaimed.

"Happened? I didn't know anything had, except the usual dreary things. This was something about a fool of a French tourist having had all his cameras and what-not stolen. You'd really think they could have sent one of the juniors along to cover a story like that, wouldn't you, particularly when Jim came in absolutely worn out after a day of chasing after those horrible ritual murder people? But for some reason Jim had to go. Just think of it. The Frenchman must be completely mental to leave anything valuable like a camera lying around in his room, because everybody, I mean everybody, knows the people here are absolute thieves——"

"Yes. Well. Thank you." Helena slammed the telephone down. She turned to Gilbert Kaggwa. "I should think you heard most of that, didn't you? And I don't suppose it would be advisable to try to telephone Mr. Passfield at the police station, so I'll try Mr. Elder." She picked up the directory again. "Have you thought what we're going to do if I can't get hold of him?"

"Try still someone else."

"But really I don't know anyone else."

"Well then, we'll think of some other way of distracting the guards."

In his calm he suddenly reminded her of Mr. Forrest, and she remembered that probably the older man had been one of the deepest influences in the life of Gilbert Kaggwa.

But Mr. Forrest had never, that she knew of, had to take the responsibility of life or death for others into his hands. Nor had anyone else that Helena had ever met. And how thankful she was for it just then, how grateful that in the normal course of her life she had never had to make up her mind how she felt about the sort of human problems posed by actually meeting, talking to, perhaps finding among one's friends, a man like this, gentle, humane, ruthless and desperate.

She dialled once more and this time, to her great relief, a man's voice answered. "Elder speaking."

"Mr. Elder, this is Helena Sebright," she began. "I'm afraid I've really no right to call you——"

"Oh, that's quite all right," he said cheerily. "It's about the job, isn't it? I was going to call you to-morrow anyway and see when we could get together about it, if you're serious about wanting to stay on. Judy Forrest said she was sure you were. Perhaps you'd have lunch with me. Could you manage to-morrow? Say at the Burton Hotel. Their food's quite decent. Judy can tell you where it is."

"Mr. Elder, this isn't anything to do with the job," Helena said. "An awful thing's happened. The police came here and found a whole lot of arms, rifles and things, buried in the Forrests' garden and they've taken Mr. and Mrs. Forrest down to the police station to get statements from them, and left me here alone. And that isn't all that's happened. This morning Jean disappeared——"

"Now wait a minute, wait a minute." His voice had changed. It had become unnaturally calm and appallingly soothing. "Let's begin again at the beginning, shall we? Take it slowly. You did say, didn't you, that the police found a lot of arms in the Forrests' garden?"

"Yes."

"But what in God's name ever made them think of looking for arms in the Forrests' garden? It seems a most unlikely spot to find such things."

"It was Wilbraham, the gardener," she said. "He hid them there and somehow the police got it out of him. And I'm here alone now, and there are guards in the garden and I can hear them prowling round the house and I'm horribly scared. And I know I oughtn't to have rung you up, but I simply don't know anyone in Tondolo, and I thought that if perhaps you could possibly come over— well, perhaps we could talk about the job while we're at it, and at least it wouldn't feel so awful as sitting here alone, listening to those footsteps outside and wondering what's happening to the Forrests and Jean. I was telling you Jean disappeared this morning, wasn't I? She went off into the blue with Cleo Grant and we were all wild with worry before this thing about the arms came up, and . . ." She pulled herself up sharply. She had been getting carried away by her own story, the tears in her voice were far from unreal, and she had almost blurted out that she had been spoken to by a kidnapper, a thing which she had no right to do until she had told the Forrests about it.

"My dear girl, of course I'll come over," Vernon Elder said. "Right away. Just hang on and don't worry. I'm sure everything will turn out all right. Someone's made a mistake, that's all. This is quite a country for that kind of mistake, but it generally gets sorted out perfectly well in the end. Everyone actually means frightfully well. So don't worry. I'm sure those footsteps don't mean anything sinister. Probably the guards are very decent chaps who are just wondering when they're going to get home to bed."

"They're armed!" Helena said quickly, in case, in his efforts to calm her down, he succeeded in calming himself so effectively that he no longer thought it necessary to come to her rescue. "And for all I know they won't let you in. But if you'd come—oh, it would be so good of you! But when you get to the gate, toot your horn, won't you? Toot it loudly—to make sure they *will* let you in, you know."

"Toot my horn—loudly?" Vernon Elder's voice had changed again. It had become the incisive voice of a man who has just understood what he is really being asked to do. "Loudly it shall be—and long, I take it. Loud and long. About ten minutes from now. And take care, my dear, whatever the trouble is."

He rang off.

Helena turned to Gilbert Kaggwa.

"You did that very well, Miss Sebright," he said. "You have the makings of a very fine actress. Thank you—thank you most sincerely."

"He'll be here in ten minutes," she said. "And it wasn't all acting."

"No, so I realised."

"I'm very frightened. I wasn't making that up. It's thinking of Jean in that man's hands. I keep hearing his voice. It was horrible. Harsh and mocking and clear, as clear as if . . ." Her own voice faltered. "As clear as if he were quite near—in Tondolo—he *is* in Tondolo, if he stole that Frenchman's cameras, and he did, he must have! The Frenchman knew the man wasn't in any of his photographs, but the man himself couldn't have been sure of that, so he had to get hold of the cameras."

"Miss Sebright, Miss Sebright!" Gilbert Kaggwa grasped her shoulder and shook it. "Now listen to me. You're helping me very much, so I'll do my best to help you. I'll give you advice, good advice. Please don't take it into your head to tackle this problem by yourself. I know how it is, you're finding it difficult to wait here, doing nothing, so you're beginning to have ideas. But please stop. Don't have ideas, don't think. Waiting is the best thing you can do for everyone. It's the best way to help the Forrests and it's safest for you——"

The telephone began to ring.

They looked at one another for an instant, then he let her go.

"Go on, answer it," he said.

She picked it up.

A faint voice checked the number, asked her who she was, said that there was a call from New York, then there was silence, except for some buzzing and singing noises on the line. Then at last there was the voice of Denis Forrest, saying remotely, "This is D-Denis. Is that you, M-Mother?"

"No, it's Helena Sebright," she answered. "I'm sorry, I'm the only person here. The others are all down at the police station."

"I s-see," he said. "Have you any n-news, Helena. Of Jean?"

She was sure that he did not see, but left him to imagine

that it was on Jean's account that his family were with
the police.

"Yes," she said. "A man rang up. He said Jean was
alive and safe. He said he'd ring again with instructions."

"Follow the instructions," he said instantly. "Do everything he asks. Everything. My mother's rich. She'll do
anything. I'm coming as quickly as I can. I don't know
when I'll arrive, but it'll be as soon as I can. Marcia too.
I telephoned her. She's leaving in the morning. Helena——"

"Yes?"

"Do everything the man tells you. Don't let them think
of anything but Jean's safety."

"No."

"We're coming as fast as we can, Marcia and I."

"Yes." She heard herself saying yes, no, yes, and thought
that there must be a hundred other things that she ought
to say. So many things that she could not pick on any one of
them, and just then, as Denis said "Good-bye," she heard
the tooting of a car's horn at the gate.

The first toot was quiet, then there was a louder and
longer one.

Gilbert Kaggwa stepped up to her while she still held
the telephone in one hand, and took her other hand between
both his own in a swift yet impressive gesture. Then on silent
feet, he vanished into the unlit dining-room. Helena had a
glimpse of him, a shadowy, white-clad sliver of a man, as he
twitched a curtain aside and slid out over the sill.

Vernon Elder's horn went on blaring away. Someone in
the garden was shouting at him.

Helena felt clammy with fear. Her heart was pounding
so that it hurt. She felt that she might be sick. But minutes
ago, while she had still been talking to Gilbert Kaggwa,
she had made up her mind what she herself had to do as soon
as he had gone.

Putting the telephone down, she went to the window
in the dining-room through which he had vanished, and followed him out in the darkness.

CHAPTER XI

There was a flowerbed under the window. She felt the soft earth under her feet as she drew back against the wall of the house and listened. The air was strongly scented by a honeysuckle that grew against the wall. Its blooms were enormous. One as big as her hand hung down almost touching her cheek.

The blackness round her seemed complete, but that was only for a moment. As her eyes grew used to it she recognised shadowy but familiar shapes of trees and bushes. Also she saw something moving between them, a slim, white figure that slipped quickly from the cover of one shrub to another, then suddenly rose a few feet in the air and vanished. Gilbert Kaggwa had climbed the garden fence and gone.

The best thing to do now was to follow him quickly. He had probably found as good a place as any for climbing the fence. And luckily for Helena, she was in black jeans and a blue shirt, which would neither show up in the dark nor get in her way. She ought to run for it while the guards were still arguing with Vernon Elder. The car horn was silent now, but she could hear the sound of voices, coming from the direction of the gate. Yet she only pressed herself harder against the wall, in the rigidity of panic. She had never been as frightened of anything as she was then of crossing the garden.

A foolish thought filled her mind. She seemed unable to think of anything else. It was of young Fitch, of the firm of Orley Fitch, smiling at her across his big desk and saying with infinite friendliness that perhaps there were human beings who were capable of being in two places at the same time, but that he didn't happen to be one of them, and please, what did she imagine he could do about it if she made an appointment for him to see a client here in the office in London on the same afternoon as he was supposed to be visiting another client in Kent?

His pleasant voice had gone on and on about it, until she had told him that the appointment in the office had been in his diary for two weeks and that he had fixed up this appointment in Kent, where she knew that he would be given a very good lunch and get in a round of golf, only two days ago without looking at the diary. Then she had left the office, gone home, gone out again, met Cleo Grant, come to Uyowa and to this moment of terror in the darkness. It was all because young Fitch liked golf a lot better than he liked doing his job.

But she couldn't stay here any longer. She must either go on or go back into the room behind her. She edged a step or two forward, felt hard-baked lawn under her feet instead of the earth of the flowerbed, and ran.

She reached the point where Gilbert Kaggwa had gone over the wooden fence. Its top was a little above the level of her eyes. It was easy enough to grasp it with her hands, but she did not know if she was going to be able to haul herself over it. She stood back a few steps, ran at the fence, grabbed the top and jumped. But there was a flowerbed in front of the fence and the earth was soft there. It took all the spring out of her leap and she flopped back on to the ground.

As she stood there, she realised that the voices at the gate had stopped. Then she heard a brief toot on the horn, like a farewell, and the car drive off. She had not much time left. Looking with hatred at the fence, she wondered why the little man in white had been able to slide over it so easily and she not. If she was not highly athletic, she was young and lightly built. Perhaps there was a bush somewhere near that would give her a foothold. She began to edge along the fence, keeping close to it, and watching the house, in case one of the guards should come wandering round it.

It was because of this that she blundered right into one of the struts that supported the fence. It projected from near the top and had its lower end buried in the midst of a clump of amaryllis, but it was itself supported by a horizontal crossbar. Helena put a foot on the crossbar, pulled herself

up, swung her legs over and lowered herself on the other side.
A burst of giggles from almost under her feet made
her nearly scream. There was a broad grassy verge to
the road here and on it, close under the fence, lay two
clasped figures. She could see almost nothing of them but
a shadowy shape, the gleam of eyeballs and the shine of
white teeth. The giggling got louder as Helena stumbled
away over the uneven grass to the pavement and something
was called after her. She did not look back but began to
walk down the hill towards the town.

At first it was really running rather than walking. Then
she thought, this won't do. Stroll, she told herself. Look
as if you're just out, walking the dog, even if there isn't a
dog. Not any more. Poor Bongo. But at all costs, look
casual. If you do, no one will bother about you any more
than that giggling couple did. Perhaps it's odd for a white
woman to be out by herself at this time of night, perhaps
they'll call things after you, but that's all there'll be to it
unless you're very unlucky.

And the police won't be bothering about you, because
they think you're safe in the house. And once you get into
the town, you can take a taxi. Oh yes, you can take a taxi,
except for that minor detail that you haven't any money.
Your handbag's lying on a table in the sitting-room, with all
your money in it, and you aren't going back for it. So
what are you going to do? Walk all the way? Yes, of
course. There isn't much choice, is there?

The long road down the hill was empty and silent. Not
even a car passed her. The people who had been on their
verandahs with their drinks and their friends when the
Forrests had driven up the road earlier in the evening,
had gone indoors. The houses were closed up, most of
them in darkness.

The street lamps lit up the gardens as well as the road,
but only in separated pools of light, with shadow between
them. Helena would have felt almost like a shadow herself
if the slap of her sandals on the pavement had not sounded
so abnormally loud to her. Passing one gateway she was
startled by a movement. For a moment she wanted to

run. But it was only a night-watchman lounging there, smoking a cigarette. He eyed her wonderingly as she went by, but said nothing.

Presently a car passed her, going up the hill, and then another. One car was full of Indians, the other of white people, returning from a party. She caught a glimpse of a sequinned dress and the flash of jewellery on one of the women inside, and saw the faces in the car turned to look at her curiously as the headlights picked her out.

There would be more traffic and more people about once she reached the main street, of course. She would get out of this deadly quietness. She was sure that it was only a respectable, suburban quietness, that there was nothing to be afraid of. If she looked over her shoulder, she would see that there was no one there. No one was going to jump at her suddenly out of the shadows. It was a superstitious and senseless fear that kept her nerves stretched as tight as she could bear and made the casualness of her walk one of the most difficult feats of her life. It would be a tremendous relief to be among traffic and people in a busy main street.

That busy main street . . .

She had forgotten that with the darkness the centre of Tondolo emptied almost as completely as the road down which she had come. The heart of the town was a place of offices and public buildings. When evening came the crowds who filled it in the daytime got into cars, buses, on to bicycles, or merely walked away, whether to their pleasant white homes on the surrounding hills, or to their hovels among the ant-hills, and the broad streets became a desert. Even if she had brought money with her, she would not have been able to find a taxi. There were no taxis to be seen.

Suddenly the voice of a drunk was uplifted in song. The song was clear and melancholy and would have been hauntingly sweet if it had not broken off in raucous laughter. Helena never saw the singer. Perhaps he had collapsed in booths in a corner, with directories on a stand alongside them, and crossed the foyer towards them. As she did some doorway. She saw a few groups of people and once two policemen came strolling along together and gave her steady stares, but took no further notice of her. She saw a few cars, but in general the place gave her the same feeling of there being a curfew in force as she had had two evenings ago, when she had driven back through the town with the Forrests from the Passfields' party.

Two evenings ago? Only two evenings?

She had hardly given a thought, since she had left the house, to Gilbert Kaggwa, or to where he had gone. He had appeared out of nowhere and melted away into darkness. There was something dreamlike about the whole encounter. She had other things to think about now. How, for instance, since she couldn't take a taxi and would have to go on walking, was she going to find her way? Whom could she ask, without its seeming unduly strange?

A possible solution to this problem presented itself to her unexpectedly as she reached a crossing and stood undecided at the corner, wondering whether to go straight on or to turn to right or left. Only a little way down the street to the left she saw the brightly lit up entrance of a biggish building, over which, in neon, were the words, "The Burton Hotel." There were several cars parked outside it and there were people in the doorway. The fact that almost opposite to the hotel there was a building with a much smaller sign which said "Police Station" was perhaps unfortunate, but not, Helena thought, any cause for serious worry. She walked to the hotel and in at the door.

At last she felt inconspicuous, for the big foyer, panelled in a sort of mosaic made of fine African timbers in a design that showed all the birds and beasts of Uyowa, was fairly full of tourists, dressed as she was in slacks, shirt and sandals, and looking almost as tired and dishevelled from some long day's bus trip as she did herself.

Mingling with them gratefully, she looked for the telephones, or rather a telephone directory, for what she needed before anything else was an address. She saw telephone so, one of the lifts came down and several people emerged from it. The first of them, in a dress of sparkling silver

jersey, with her blued hair as smooth as burnished steel, was
the American woman who had been in the bus party
at Ross Falls.

Helena changed her plans at that moment. With luck
there need be no long walk through the silent dark. If
she could borrow some money from this woman, who had
seemed so warm-hearted and already knew part of her
troubles, she could go to the clerk at the Inquiries desk
and ask him how to hire a car in this town. It might take
a little time, of course, explaining to the woman how
she came to be out like this without any money of her
own, but not as long, surely, as going the rest of the way
on foot. She could say that she needed the car to get
home. Meanwhile, of course, she still needed that address.
She went on towards the telephones. But she kept an eye
on the American woman, for if she was going out, Helena
would have to run after her and catch her before she
vanished.

The woman was not going out. She was only looking
for the cocktail bar. As soon as she spotted the sign that
pointed the way, she walked off down the corridor towards
it. Helena started turning the pages of a directory.

There was the address, 27 Lukulu Avenue. She turned
to go to the Inquiries desk.

A man stood in her way. Big, pink-faced, bald. The
Norwegian who had been in the bus party.

"Ah, now I have the chance to ask you if you have any
news of the little girl," he said. "We have heard of the terrible tragedy to the young lady who was with her. She
is believed to have fallen in the river, no? We heard
this before we started back to Tondolo. But of the little
girl nothing definite was known yet."

His pink face was all concern. There was earnest sympathy
in his light blue eyes. But Helena stared at him in horror.
She was taken utterly by surprise. For hadn't it been that
voice, with its heavy foreign accent, that had spoken to
her only a little while ago over the telephone? Had told
her that he would ring again with "instructions"? Made its
cruel joke, laughed?

The man saw the horror on her face and said quickly, "Forgive me if I have intruded. I did not mean it. I wished only to ask—to say I hope—you have some good news—to express sympathy, I beg your pardon. I see I should not have spoken. A stranger—I cannot help."

His pink face had turned red with embarrassment.

The breath that Helena had been holding escaped with a choking rasp. It was not the telephone voice at all. It was too deep, the intonation was quite different. She was as certain of that now as for that shocked moment she had been certain that it was the voice.

"I'm sorry," she said. "I—it's all been a great strain. I'm afraid I'm not quite myself. You're very kind."

"Then you have news," he said. "Bad news."

"None at all," she answered.

"That perhaps is hardest of all. But you can still hope. I go now to meet Mrs. Jackson, the American lady, in the cocktail bar for a drink. Perhaps I may invite you to join us."

"Thank you, but——" Helena checked herself in the middle of her refusal. "Thank you, I'd like to very much. There's a problem—if I could tell you about it—but there's something I'd just like to ask about first at Inquiries. I'll follow you in a moment."

"Good, good," he said. "Any help I can give, please ask. The same, I am sure, for Mrs. Jackson. She has been most distressed all day by what we heard. I expect you then in the cocktail bar in a few minutes."

"Yes. Thank you."

He walked away and Helena went towards the Inquiries desk.

Crossing the big foyer, she was saying to herself, "27 Kukulu Avenue. No, that wasn't it, that's wrong. Kuluku Avenue. No. Lukuku. No. Oh God, I'll have to go back and look it up again, and even if the clerk manages to have a car here ready and waiting to take me there by the time I've managed to borrow some money from those people, it's all wasting time, and time probably matters

F

more than anything else now! Lukulu—that was it! 27 Lukulu Avenue."

She went up to the desk and lent her elbows on the broad, polished counter.

When the clerk turned to her she asked, "Can you tell me where Lukulu Avenue is?"

"Yes, yes." He was an elderly African, with the African habit of saying most things at least twice. He brought a map out from under the counter and spread it out before her. "You go here—and here—and here—and there you are. You see."

"Yes," she said, concentrating. "Thank you. Now, I was thinking of hiring a car. . . ."

"Why, Miss Sebright." The rich, plummy voice of Jim Passfield broke in from just behind her. He and the Frenchman who had had his cameras stolen had just come into the hotel together. "Really, of all people in the world, you're about the last I was expecting to meet here. I've just popped over from the police station, for a drink with Monsieur Barbier, and I heard all about the Forrests' trouble while I was there, naturally. Scandalous business taking them in like that. Nothing to worry about, of course. I mean, they'll be letting them go again any time now. It was just a bit of sabre-rattling. But I thought the police had you safely sewed up at home. I never thought I'd find you wandering around down here. How did you manage it? Or was I given the story wrong? Wouldn't surprise me. Nothing surprises me much any more, unless it's being told the truth about something for a change."

"You've seen the Forrests?" Helena asked.

"Only briefly," he said. "I actually went down to the police station because of a message from the paper about Monsieur Barbier having his camera—all his cameras and films and everything—stolen. Valuable stuff. And I just saw the Forrests through an open door, and asked the chaps I was talking to what the hell. They told me a lot of stuff about arms in the Forrests' garden, then remembered I work for a paper and clammed up. Said nothing was for publication as yet, though there was a great story brewing. Then they all looked very knowing and told me not to try prowling around up there myself, as there were guards in the garden. That was when I gathered you were up there alone."

"Well, I was," Helena said, "and I didn't much like it, so I came down into the town."

"My God, how?"

"Oh, there wasn't any special difficulty about it," she lied smoothly.

"But the guards in the garden—aren't there any guards there?" he asked.

"Oh yes, but they weren't bothering much about me. They were left there to stop people going in, not coming out. And I'd only been left behind to take the call from Denis Forrest, if he rang up from New York, so once he had, I walked down here. I—I wanted to tell the Forrests about Denis's call, but they wouldn't let me in at the police station and——"

The clerk behind the desk interrupted, "Madam, you were asking about hiring a car, madam. . . ."

"A car?" Jim Passfield said. "D'you want to go somewhere? Let me take you. Car's at the door."

"That's awfully kind of you," Helena said, "only I'd hate to bother you. I could hire a car, I'm sure, and——"

"No trouble, no trouble at all. Where are you going?"

She had to take a decision quickly. She had to act on it immediately. It meant taking a big risk, then trusting to improvisation.

"Well, as a matter of fact, I was just going home," she said.

"Nothing simpler, then. Let's go." He turned to the Frenchman. "Good night, Barbier. I'm damned sorry about the cameras and all and I'll try to see the story gets plenty of publicity, but I don't hold out much hope you'll see any of your stuff again. Glad at any rate you're fully insured——"

"Insured!" cried the Frenchman. "Yes, my cameras are insured. My lenses are insured. I can get the same again, or better. But my pictures, Mr. Passfield—how can one insure pictures? All I have taken—yes, every single photograph I have taken since I left Paris—gone! And perhaps I shall never come here again. In all my life, never again. And I have not a picture of it left to show I have been here. It is the pictures that matter. You say that when you write about it, please. Tell the thief he may keep my cameras and my lenses. He may have them all and I will not prosecute if only he will put my films in the post and return them to me. They are not of any conceivable use to him, but to me they mean so much. I am almost ashamed to say how much. Please ask this thief to return my pictures to me!"

"Of course," Jim Passfield said. "I'll do the best I can, but honestly, I shouldn't build on it. The cameras have probably been flogged by now and the films thrown on some scrapheap. I'd go and have a drink, if I were you, and do my best to forget the whole unfortunate business. Now, Miss Sebright——"

He took her arm and they went out through the doorway to the street.

"I really don't like to trouble you like this," she said. "You've had a long day, haven't you?"

"A bloody long day—a bloody long two days, as a matter of fact," he answered. "And didn't get much for my trouble either, chasing around in the footsteps of Robbie Meldrum, who never tells one anything anyway, even if one does catch up with him. We were up in the north, trying to pick up some information about some murders in a village there. Ritual murders, witch doctor stuff, you know. Thirteen murders, the number of the witch's coven the world over. Isn't that interesting? Very nasty, all the same, because, apart from anything else, to our minds they seem quite motiveless."

"Does that make it worse?"

They were walking along the pavement to where his car was parked. He walked with long steps for such a short, stocky man, with his heavy shoulders hunched so that his head looked sunk between them. His plump cheeks

sagged with fatigue, but the gaze that he turned on Helena
was alert and questioning.

"You think it doesn't?"

"I think the more nearly rational it seems, the worse it
is," she said.

"Now that's interesting," he said. "I've always put it
the other way round. The more rational the motive, the
nearer the murder gets to—well, warfare, revolution, and
other normal human activities."

"Are warfare and revolution normal?"

"Well, aren't they? Look around you. We're practically
in the middle of a revolution here and now. Anything
could blow up at any time. You may not have realised it,
but I know this place so well, I can smell it in the air.
And a lot more than thirteen people will be killed and
you may have a glimpse of their bodies on television, with
armoured cars going up and down the street, and have a
moment of shock, because even on television the dead look
so very dead, but then you'll forget about them. But you
won't forget those thirteen ritual murders in a village you've
never heard of."

Or one, a single one, that happened at Ross Falls, Helena
thought. A movement too near the edge of the precipice,
a sudden push, a cry drowned in the roar of the water,
then death among the rocks below, and nothing left even to
look dead on television. Committed for gain, generally
considered, the most rational of all motives.

"I don't think you make normality sound particularly
attractive," she said. "If I thought you were right, I'd take
abnormality any time. But actually I don't think either word
has any meaning."

"I expect you're right. We do throw them both around
rather carelessly. And if you want to say that war and
revolution are only ritual murder on a large scale, I shan't
argue with you about that either."

They had reached his car. He unlocked it and held the
door open for Helena. She got in. He slammed the door shut,
walked round the car, got into the driving seat and pushed
the key into the ignition.

At that moment Helena cried out, "Oh look—wait—
there's Mr. Meldrum!" She was twisted in her seat, looking
through the rear window of the car.

"Meldrum?" Jim Passfield said with a puzzled frown.
"It can't be. Where?"

"He's just gone into the hotel."

"But he isn't back yet. I was in the police station with
Barbier and they said——"

"But he came out of the police station," Helena said ex-
citedly. "And perhaps he can tell me something about the
Forrests—what they're doing to them. I must get hold
of him. Wait!"

"Wait—I'll go," Jim Passfield said and got quickly out of
the car. "If it was Meldrum, I'll bring him along."

He went trotting off along the pavement back to the
hotel.

Helena waited until he reached its entrance, then she slid
into the driving seat, switched on the ignition and took
the grey Vauxhall gently out from the row along the curb
and on down the street.

CHAPTER XII

This was the first time that Helena had ever stolen a car and it had gone off exactly as she had planned. A feeling of exhilaration made her almost forget for the moment why she had done it. She did not accelerate until after she had turned the corner, but then she speeded up along the empty road ahead. She had never driven this make of car before, but she was a good driver and in a few minutes felt at ease with the unfamiliar controls. Lucky, she thought, that all the roads of Tondolo were so empty at this time of night; lucky too that in Uyowa they still stuck to the British habit of driving on the left side of the road. She found the way easier to remember than she had expected. It was not only that her glimpse of the map at the Inquiries desk in the hotel had been useful, but she found that actually she had taken in more of the route the other evening than she had realised.

How long had she before Jim Passfield realised that there was no Robbie Meldrum in the hotel and came to tell her so and found his car had gone?

Probably only a few minutes. But with the total absence of taxis in the streets of Tondolo, it was unlikely that he would be able to follow her at once. Unless by any chance he ran straight into some friend who would drive him after her, he would have to get that old clerk to call him a hired car. And possibly, in the circumstances, he might not be too keen on seeking the help of a friend.

In the circumstances. And suppose she was all wrong about the circumstances. . . .

The moment of uncertainty did not make her slow down. The headlights lit up the lovely colours of the flowers that lined the sides of the street, making them jewel-bright for an instant before they vanished back into shadow. There was not a car in sight behind her. No one was following her yet. She had at least a little time in hand.

When she turned the car in at the gate of the Passfields' house, 27 Lukulu Avenue, she was greeted by the warning barking of a dog. It was the deep, baying bark of a big dog. She remembered him now, a long-legged creature of uncertain breed with small pointed ears, a strong square muzzle and heavy shoulders. He had stalked about among the guests, looking them over suspiciously and not responding at all to friendly overtures.

Driving up to the door, Helena stopped the car, but did not get out till she had made sure where the barking was coming from. Yes, there the dog was on the prowl in the garden. But the familiar car with the unfamiliar driver was puzzling him. He came slowly toward it, the hairs standing up along his spine and the barking changing to a low, uncertain growling.

Helena pressed on the horn and kept her hand there.

A light went on on the verandah. There were other lights on in the house, but all the windows were screened by venetian blinds. After a moment the door on to the verandah opened a few inches and Peg Passfield peered out. She recognised the car and called out, "Jim?" Then she shouted at the dog, "Jerk, you stupid beast, what's got into you? Jerk, come here!"

The dog stood its ground and continued to growl.

"Jerk, will you do as I tell you?" she yelled at him. "Come here, you brute!"

Unwillingly the dog obeyed her. She turned back into the house, leaving the door open behind her.

"He knows you're afraid of him, that's the trouble," she said over her shoulder with a contemptuous laugh. "They aren't fools, dogs, like some people. How did it go?"

Helena had got quietly out of the car and walked up the steps of the verandah.

"It went pretty well, I believe, if you mean stealing the photographs," she said. "On the other hand, it wasn't necessary."

Peg Passfield whirled round at the sound of her voice. She was in yellow pyjamas, her hair was on rollers and her face was covered in night cream. Under its oily shine her sharp little features went papery white.

"How did you get here?" She rushed to the door and shouted out into the darkness, "Jim! Jim, where are you?"

The dog leapt past her and Helena into the garden barking wildly again. Helena shouldered Peg Passfield back into the house and slammed the door.

"He isn't here." Helena leant against the door, feeling behind her for the key in the lock, turned the key and slipped it into her pocket. "I took the car and came by myself. Where's Jean?"

Peg Passfield's eyes became enormous in her terrified face.

"Jean? Who's Jean?" She was walking slowly backwards as Helena advanced towards her. "I don't know any Jean?"

'She's here," Helena said. "That's why you had to get rid of your servants. You couldn't keep her here with them in the house."

"I got rid of my servants because they were stupid clots who made me go screaming mad," Peg Passfield answered.

"I think you're screaming mad already," Helena said and suddenly leapt forward and knocked Peg Passfield aside from the desk towards which she had been retreating. Her hand had just been reaching for the handle of a drawer. Helena pulled it open. Inside it lay a revolver.

Unfortunately, she knew nothing about revolvers. She had never shot at anything with any kind of weapon since she had stopped, a good many years ago, finding water pistols amusing. But she took the revolver gingerly out of the drawer, at which Peg began to laugh hysterically.

"It isn't loaded, you fool. You can't frighten me with it. Get out of my house! I'd get out very fast if I were you, before Jim gets here."

"Not loaded?" To make sure of it, Helena raised the revolver, pointed it, roughly speaking, at a gilt framed mirror on the wall, and pulled the trigger. There was a click and that was all. "Fine, then I *can* use it." She changed her grip on the revolver, grasping it by the barrel. Swinging it slightly, she took a step towards Peg. "Where's

Jean? Take me to her. Get on with it, or I'm going to get very, very rough with you."

Helena knew as she spoke that she would not really be capable of using the gun on the other woman. If it came to the point, she would throw it away and fly at Peg with her natural weapons, hands and nails and teeth and kicking feet. She had the sort of anger in herself that would make that possible, but to feel the cold metal in her hand striking warm flesh would only weaken her.

Peg Passfield had backed to the wall now and stood there with her hands flattened against it.

"You're crazy," she said. "You're insane. You're danger-ous. You ought to be put away."

"Where's Jean?" Helena repeated.

For once anger was not making her voluble. It seemed to have reduced her vocabulary to two words.

"Jean, Jean!—where's Jean?" Peg Passfield mimicked her. Her eyes gleamed mockingly. "How should I know where Jean is? You're the person who ought to know. You're the person who was supposed to be taking care of her."

"Listen," Helena said, forcing herself to speak slowly, instead of seizing the other woman by the neck and shaking an answer out of her. "Listen, for your own sake. Your husband's name isn't Passfield, is it? It's Petrzelka. He came here from the Congo, where he'd an agency of some sort. Wasn't it a news agency? Wasn't he a journalist? That brilliant future Cleo Grant believed he was going to have, wasn't that going to be as a writer? And I suppose he'd got hold of a British passport somehow—a forged one, perhaps, I don't know. And at some stage in his career he picked up that perfect English he speaks. It *is* perfect except that his accent is just a little too careful. It's just too good to be true. And he can shed it when he wants to, as he did when he spoke to me on the telephone. And he married you because he believed the story you were telling people when you first came here about how rich you were——"

"Stop it!" Peg Passfield's pale face turned crimson. "Stop

it, it's all untrue! He'll tell you it's untrue when he gets here. He'll get here soon even if you did steal his car."

"And what will he do then?" Helena asked. "The same as he did to Cleo Grant? Hasn't it occurred to you you may get the same treatment too? He won't want to be encumbered with you when he takes off for that bolt-hole he's planned all along."

"Stop it! Stop it!"

"I expect it's what he intended for you from the start," Helena went on, "even when he was making you help him, making you give that party that was to get us all out of the way so that Cleo could get into the Forrests' house and arrange things with Jean, and making you look after her for him till he got the money from the Forrests. You knew all about Cleo, of course. You knew she'd written to him telling him that Jean was coming and that here was a chance for him to make his fortune and go off with her, leaving you. And you knew that he was going to trick Cleo. You did, didn't you? You knew he was going to use her to lay a conspicuous false trail away from Tondolo and then get rid of her. So you're an accessory to murder as well as to kidnapping, and you haven't much chance now unless you help me. *Where's Jean?*"

The colour that had flared in Peg Passfield's face had faded. Her small, pallid mouth was pinched. Suddenly she sprang forward and kicked at Helena savagely, then twisted away from her and fled into the kitchen. With a fire of pain in the knee where Peg's pointed slipper had struck, Helena ran after her. A door into the garden was open and Peg in her yellow pyjamas went running across the lawn.

She shouted, "Jerk! Jerk!"

The exciting barking of the big dog answered her.

Helena slammed the door shut, locked it and shot the bolts. Then for a moment she had to lean against it as wave after wave of dizziness almost washed out consciousness. She was aware of thinking with a strange sort of coolness that she was not very good at violence, that perhaps she ought to practise more. Then she found herself clinging hard to the handle of the door and wondering how she had got there. She was panting and felt clammy all over.

The dog was snarling just outside the door. She moved away from it, found that she was steadier on her feet than she felt, went back into the sitting-room and up the stairs.

There were five doors on the landing, one that led into a bathroom, another into a big double bedroom and a third into a small room, furnished as a sort of study. These were all standing open. Helena only glanced into each room. Then she tried the handle of the nearer of the two closed doors. It opened into a closet, full of linen and blankets. She tried the second closed door. This was locked. But the key was in the lock and she had only to turn it to open the door. Her hand went out to the key, but then all of a sudden froze. For the first time since she had come into the house she asked herself if the worst shock of all of the last two days might not be waiting for her here.

Very gently, as if she were afraid of waking someone in the room, she turned the key and edged the door open.

There was darkness inside. She felt for the light switch and pressed it. She saw a small bedroom, sparsely furnished. A guest-room, rather dusty, for guests who probably did not come very often. And Jean was there, still in her jeans and red shirt. She was lying on her back on the bed with her eyes closed and her mouth open. Her colour was ashen, and her breathing rasped a little.

Uncontrollable tears of relief began to pour out of Helena's eyes. Unconscious of dropping the revolver on the floor, she flung herself down on her knees by the bed and tried to take the child in her arms. Then she discovered that the way that Jean was lying, with her arms up across the pillow, was because her wrists were tied to the bedposts. With a new rage blazing inside her at the sight of the small, helpless hands and the heavy cords round the narrow wrists, Helena began to tug at the knots.

As she did so, Jean's eyes opened. They did not recognise Helena. They only gave her a dull stare out of the dark abyss of a nightmare, then closed again.

It was at that moment that Helena heard the first shots fired in the town.

They sounded far nearer than the firing that she had heard from the Forrests' house on the first morning of her visit. There was silence after them, then another crackle of sound, that seemed to be coming from several places at the same time. Then came an explosion that made the house shiver. Before its echoes had died away there came another.

Helena's first impulse had been to run to the window, to pull back the curtains and look out. But checking it, she went on wrestling with the knotted cords. She freed one of Jean's wrists fairly easily, but the other was more securely tied. She was still pulling at the cord when she remembered something. The key of the room was still on the outside of the door. Getting up quickly, she went to it, opened it a few inches and took the key from the lock, shut the door again and locked it on the inside. As she did it she heard the rattle of more firing which sounded closer at hand.

A moment afterwards she heard the crash of breaking glass. That was the sound that she had been expecting. It meant that Peg Passfield had smashed a window and was back in her own house.

What would she do now? If she had a grain of sense, even the smallest regard for her own safety, she would grab some clothes and some money and drive away in the car that was still at the door, would drive out of the town, away from the firing, and away, as far and as fast as she could, from the man who would show her no more mercy than he had Cleo Grant. Petrzelka was a man who did not care to carry excess baggage in the way of women who were useless to him, and what use was Peg now?

Helena supposed that he might still extort money from the Forrests by promising to return Jean unharmed to them, but as things had worked out, he would have to kill Helena and probably Jean too, whether or not he obtained the money, and that meant that any hope he had had of continuing his comfortable life here was ended. And it was only if he wanted to do that, to go on being Jim Passfield, the pleasant fellow who worked on the local paper, who had so many friends and was welcome everywhere, that Peg was any use to him. But Helena believed that he had never intended to stay. Once he had the money, she was sure, he had always meant to disappear quietly into the vast confusion that was Africa, to start a new, free life under a new name, perhaps to find a new and really rich wife this time, while Peg's body was left to rot rapidly away in the tropical heat, in some ditch or river into which he had thrown it from the car.

Helena was listening intently. After the breaking of the glass, there were no sounds in the house. It was quiet outside too. Even the dog was quiet. She did not like it. She had gone back to Jean's bedside, untied the second cord and started gently rubbing the two small wrists. The cord had left a rope-like pattern on them, but otherwise appeared to have done no harm. Helena thought that Jean must already have been deeply drugged by the time that she had been tied to the bedposts and had not struggled. The cords had only been a precaution in case she recovered consciousness before the Passfields were ready to do whatever they had intended next.

Suddenly, not far away, there were a few shots, an outburst of shouting and screaming, a few more shots, then again silence. Then there was another explosion. Through a chink in the curtains, Helena saw bright light outside the window instead of darkness.

She went to the window, parted the curtains a few inches and looked out. A house only a little way down the hill into the town was on fire. It was not the only fire to be seen. There were several, dotted about the hillsides round the town, and in the middle of it a great blaze flared upwards, turning the sky above it to a sultry bronze. The rattle of shooting was becoming continuous.

But in the house there was still complete silence.

Helena's unease because of it grew. She tried to visualise what Peg Passfield was doing. Was she sitting rigid in some corner, immobilised by terror as the fighting grew fiercer? Was she merely waiting calmly for the return of

her husband? But would he be able to return through the
turmoil developing in the town? Even if he dared to drive
through it, would the fighters in the streets let him through?
Wasn't he probably stuck somewhere in the midst of the
uproar? That was a cheering thought. It promised Helena
a little time to think, to plan an escape.

But then it occurred to her that perhaps he had returned
already, that when she had heard the breaking of the window
downstairs, both the Passfields had climbed in together, and
that the reason for the silence now was simply that the two
of them were sitting down there, quietly discussing what
to do, since the appearance of Helena on the scene had
somewhat upset their plans. There was an extra killing to be
done, an extra body to dispose of.

If there had been any heavy furniture in the room, Helena
would have pushed it in front of the door. But there was
no wardrobe, only a built-in wall cupboard. The dressing-
table was a flimsy affair. The bed was the solidest thing
there. It had a heavy metal frame and thick wooden ends. If
she moved it across the doorway, it might prevent the door
being simply pushed in if the lock were smashed. Then,
if she lifted the dressing-table on to the bed and added
the one small arm-chair in the room, the total would be
pretty heavy. And a barricade that lasted even for a short time
might save her life and Jean's. It might make just enough
delay for someone to discover their whereabouts and come
to their rescue. Not that help from the police was to be expected on a night like this. They would have other things
on their minds. But you had to go on hoping. She stooped
to lift Jean off the bed.

Somewhere in the house there was a fearful scream.

There was just the one scream, then silence again. There
had been nothing before it, no shots, no shouts, no sound
of a car coming, no trampling in the garden. There was
nothing afterwards either. Only the lengthening silence.
Then the dog began to howl.

Outside there was silence at that moment, an eerie pause
in the growing battle, as if the giant of destruction needed
a slight rest to get his breath. Helena returned to the

window and looked out. The blaze in the centre of the town was even bigger than before. The sky over it looked red-hot. There were more small fires dotted about the hillsides surrounding it. Over the nearest she could see the sparks dancing gaily and beautifully above the curling flames. She wondered who had lived in the house. Had they died in it or fled in time? Had they been enemies of one side or the other, or merely quiet people whose home was being burnt because of the wild joy it had given to some roving, aimless crowd to light a big fire?

And where were the Forrests? Still in the middle of the town, or had they got home? Was their home one of the quivering points of light that she could see on the distant hillside?

But she was losing time. Turning back to the bed, Helena picked Jean up and laid her down on the carpet beside it, put the pillow under her head, then began to push the bed towards the door. It was certainly heavy and its casters were small and old, moving reluctantly across the carpet. She had it only half-way to the door when she heard a sound outside in the passage. Suddenly the key in the lock fell out on to the floor.

She jumped and stood still, staring. A wire came through the keyhole. It twisted this way and that, then was withdrawn. While the dog still howled, a voice began to speak through the keyhole. It was a quiet, smooth, plummy, friendly voice.

"Now, Miss Sebright, please let us handle this difficult situation in a reasonable manner," it said. "I want no harm to come to you or the child. I'm not at all a violent man. I've never in my life intended any harm to anyone——"

"What was that scream?" Helena interrupted.

"What scream?" he asked.

"A few minutes ago. A ghastly scream."

" 'I heard the owl hoot and the cricket cry,' " he answered with a little chuckle. "I also heard some shooting and some bombs going off. Perhaps that distracted my attention."

"Have you killed your wife?"

"Miss Sebright, you do ask the most extraordinary ques-

tions. And do the most extraordinary things, if I may say
so. Stealing my car. I had to borrow a bicycle to get home—
that was all I could get at short notice—and had to pedal all
the way up this fearful hill. I haven't really got my breath
back even yet. You know, I never dreamt what you had in
mind. I'm a simple soul, you see. Unsuspicious. It was really
very clever, though. But it would have been cleverer still if
it had occurred to you that a desperate character like me
would probably have a gun handy. It was in the glove
compartment of the car. You could have helped yourself
to it so easily. But I've got it now and it would be the
simplest thing in the world for me to shoot this lock out.
But you or the child might be harmed while I was doing it,
and I should be so sorry about that. So why don't you open
the door, so that we can talk the situation over more
comfortably? I swear I don't mean you any harm."

"No more than you meant Cleo Grant."

"Cleo? But that was an utter accident, Miss Sebright. She
went too near the edge and she slipped."

"It's easy to slip when you're pushed."

"But this is terrible, Miss Sebright," he exclaimed.
"You're utterly wrong about me. I'm not that sort of person
at all. I was going to return Jean to her grandparents
completely safe and sound. That's why I brought her back
to Tondolo, of course, instead of getting rid of her at
the Falls, where it would have been so easy."

"Wasn't it really because you thought her grandparents
might demand some proof she was still alive before paying
the ransom?"

"I assure you, if you hadn't come here interfering, I'd
have returned her without harming a hair of her head. Now,
of course, the question of just how we're to arrange it is a
good deal more difficult. But I think we might still work
something out if you'd be a little co-operative."

"By opening the door and letting you come in and shoot
us in comfort." Helena gave a heave to the bed and moved
it nearer to the door. "I know you've got to shoot us now.
Whatever I promised in the way of silence, you'd know
you couldn't trust it."

"There is that, of course. But the child doesn't have to be killed, you know. She saw me at the Falls, but I don't think she'd recognise me again. I had on a hat with a drooping brim and dark spectacles. And she's been heavily doped ever since. So in case you should think her life's of some importance, mightn't we at least talk?"

Helena gave another heave to the bed. "I think my own life's of importance too," she said. "And I don't think you mean to let either of us go."

He gave a queer little giggle, his first departure from the normal manner of Jim Passfield.

"Well, of course, it's an almost perfect night for the disposal of bodies," he said. "There are going to be a good many lying around by the morning. Police inquiries into how this or that person got shot are not going to be very searching. There's fire too, wonderful for the obliterating of traces."

The bed was across the doorway now. Helena began to pull the light dressing-table towards it.

Perhaps he heard it, for his voice went up into a fierce shout. "Let me in! You're right I'm going to kill you, but it may make some difference to how I do it. And I'm not going to kill the child. I tell you, I'm not going to kill her. You're right, I need her alive. If she gets killed now, it's your fault."

As he spoke, he fired twice quickly at the lock.

There was a splintering sound, a little whine in the room, as if a mosquito had momentarily started to buzz, and a dull slap into the plaster of the wall opposite the door. Helena ran to Jean and pushed her into a corner of the room against the wall in which the door itself was set. Jean half-awoke, her eyelids fluttering up.

"Helena," she mumbled in a puzzled way, then sighed deeply and went back into unconsciousness.

"Helena!" someone else shouted. "Helena, are you here? Helena, if you're here, answer me!"

"I'm here!" Her voice sounded fantastically loud in her own ears, as if it had taken on some of the resonance of another explosion that came just then on the hillside. Yet perhaps to anyone else, she thought, the roar of the bomb drowned her cry. As the rattle of noises that followed the crash subsided, she shouted again, "Paul, I'm up here. But he's got a gun—Paul, do you hear, he's got a gun!"

"I've got a gun too," Paul called out. "And I'm coming up, Petrzelka—Jim—I'm coming up."

He was answered by a shot and by the furious barking of the dog.

But Helena heard no cry, no thud of a body falling, only more shots. She did not know how many, or from which direction they were coming, for she had gone to kneel on the floor beside Jean, between her and the door, and as she crouched there the sounds from the passage suddenly seemed remote and vague and unimportant. It was fireworks night, she thought. November the fifth. Everyone in the world was letting off fireworks. Outside and inside. And they had lit great fires everywhere to burn the guy who had tried to destroy parliament.

But that was in another country. . . .

She fought off the reeling images, and sat back on her heels, listening.

There were no more shots in the house, and the dog was silent. There was only the sound of running feet and the slam of a door. Outside the night was quiet again. The giant was having another rest to get his breath. In the silence a car started up, swung out into the road and accelerated wildly down the hill.

She went back to the door and called, "Paul?"

There was no answer for a moment and a chill of renewed terror froze her. Then she heard Paul's voice, almost insanely matter-of-fact, replying from downstairs, "It's all right, Helena. Nothing to worry about. He's gone. I'll be up in a moment. There's just—something here I want to deal with first."

"Jean's here," she called.

He did not reply, but a moment later she heard his footsteps on the stairs.

But of course, she realised, when he reached the door, he would not be able to get in. The bed was across the doorway. She looked at it with a sort of wonder, and at the dressing-table that she had started to pull towards it.

What a futile idea her barricade had been. As if it would have kept Petrzelka out for more than a minute or two. Trying to build it up had just been a way of deceiving herself that she was doing something useful. But now it was in Paul's way. She started to drag the heavy bedstead back from the doorway.

When she had moved the bed only a little way, he managed to edge his way into the room round the half-open door. There was blood on his face from a gash above his temple, but he seemed unaware of it.

He said, "She's dead—Peg—he killed her by sticking a spear into her. A thing they had up on the wall. He stuck it into her throat. I wanted to cover her before I came up. I didn't want you or Jean to see her. The dog's dead too."

He came round the end of the bed.

Only then he seemed to take in why it was there and why the dressing-table was in the middle of the room. It seemed to strike him as funny. He gave a rather foolish-sounding little laugh. Helena found herself echoing it. It was the aftermath of shock in which people do things of which they are totally unaware, that in themselves have no meaning. Then she went into his arms and they clung to one another.

CHAPTER XIII

It was only when he saw the blood that got smeared on to Helena's face from his that Paul seemed to realise that he was bleeding. Pulling a handkerchief out of his pocket, he dabbed absently at the long cut on his forehead as he went across the room to Jean, and knelt beside her. He felt her pulse, lifted an eyelid, looked closely at one of her limp arms. There was a shuddering, almost convulsive change from anxiety to relief on his face.

"It's all right," he said. "They've given her several shots, but she's in quite good shape. She'll sleep it off."

Helena stood in the middle of the room, watching him as he picked Jean up, laid her on the bed and covered her.

"How did he get away?" Helena asked. "Jim Passfield. Petrzelka."

Blood was slithering down Paul's cheek again. A drop splashed on to the pillow. He pressed the handkerchief back against the gash.

"One of the rooms has a balcony, I think. He probably got down a trellis. Does it matter? On a night like this he probably won't get far."

"How did you get here?" Helena asked.

"It was luck, mostly. My windscreen's a mess. They shot at the car for no particular reason when I was passing a house they'd set on fire. There was some looting going on and a lot of people were trigger-happy. That's when I got this." He tapped his forehead. "A piece of flying glass. Passfield didn't get me. He only got the dog as it was going for me."

"Hadn't we better do something about you?" she said. "They may have disinfectant and some bandages somewhere. I'll go and look."

"All right, but don't go downstairs," he said. "I covered her, but ... Well, don't go down."

Between them they moved the bed away from the door to its old position and Helena went out into the passage and into the bathroom. In the cabinet there she found a bottle of disinfectant and some Band-aid.

Bringing them back to Paul, she said, "I expect you can make a better job of this than I can."

He was sitting on the edge of the bed with one of Jean's hands in his. He looked up with a smile.

"Sympathetic, aren't you? I think the patient would enjoy some attention."

"Tell me what to do then."

Under his directions, she cleaned and dressed the cut. While she was doing it, she said, "How did you find us?"

"I talked to the Frenchman, Barbier. I saw him in the hotel after the police let us go. They'd kept us hanging around in a futile sort of way, then all of a sudden, when the trouble in the town started up, they wanted to get rid of us as fast as they could, so we went straight over to the hotel, as that seemed safer than trying to drive home, and the place seemed probably fairly fireproof. There was a big fire going already in the poorer Indian quarter, where a lot of the houses are wooden. . . ." He took both her hands as she finished pressing the dressing in place, and rested his forehead on them.

"Helena, my love," he said.

She knelt on the floor in front of him and rested her own head against his.

He went on, "Remember my telling you, the day I fetched you from the airport, that some of the things that happen here aren't pretty? I saw some things to-night . . . But nothing quite as horrible as what I found downstairs. That poor damned woman."

"I'm only a very little bit sorry for her," Helena said. "She knew what she was doing. She helped very willingly. She only didn't understand her own real place in the scheme."

"Well, as I was saying, Barbier told me you'd left the hotel with Jim Passfield. He said Passfield had offered to drive you home. So there was the problem of what you were doing in the hotel at all when you were supposed to be up at the house—the problem of what you were up to. And I'd already begun to think about Passfield, first because of that party they asked us to, the only time when Cleo could have got into the house and made her arrangements with Jean. And she couldn't have chosen that evening by chance, she must have known we'd all be out. Then the Frenchman having his photographs stolen meant that that man in the car above Ross Falls must be here in Tondolo. And I remembered mother saying that Peg Passfield had suddenly got rid of all her servants, which didn't sound like her—I mean to have got rid of them before she'd got others to take over ..."

"Yes, that's more or less how I thought myself," Helena said. "But d'you know what I can't understand, Paul? Why did Cleo ever bring me in on the scheme? She can't have thought I'd be a help."

"Oh, because Marcia would never have let Jean come at all without someone to bring her back. Marcia never thought of distrusting Cleo, but she deeply distrusted my mother. What I personally can't understand is that that man—Jim Passfield, whom we all thought of, I suppose, as a bit of a clown—should have been the one man Cleo ever managed to love. I told you she saw him as strong and brilliant and witty."

"You also said he was stateless and homeless—dependent on her. She was always great for helping people who weren't much worth helping. Which reminds me, Gilbert Kaggwa described himself to me as a very harmless, helpless man. To look outside, it doesn't seem quite true, does it?"

"Kaggwa?" Paul said quickly. "When have you seen Kaggwa?"

She told him. She also told him of his brother's call from New York and of the call from the kidnapper.

In the middle of it Paul stood up and went to the window and looked out. The quiet had continued for some time now, except for a few distant bursts of shooting, but the sky was still red from the fires in the town. They would burn on for hours.

"Kaggwa there for two days in our house," Paul said wonderingly at last. "If we'd known it we might have helped him."

"It doesn't much look as if he needs help." Helena said.

"Oh, this isn't Kaggwa's doing," Paul said. "I think it's the army again, using the general unrest as an excuse to take over completely. I shouldn't be surprised if both Kaggwa and Mukasa are dead by now, if they didn't get out of the town in time. God, I wish we'd known Kaggwa was there. We liked him. We'd never have turned him in. And then Josiah and the others needn't have helped Cleo to get Jean out of the way and lied to us about it."

"He didn't want to involve you." Helena joined him at the window. "What do we do now, Paul? Wait here?"

"Yes, at least till daylight. If things have stayed quiet till then, we might try making for home."

"Is there any way we could let your parents know Jean's safe?"

"I'll try the telephone, but I'll be surprised if it's working."

He went out to try the telephone in the small study across the passage, but as he had expected, the line was dead. When he was out on the landing, however, he discovered the linen cupboard and when he returned to the bedroom he had an armful of blankets.

"You're going to have a rest now, and you'd probably sooner have it in here than in the Passfields' bedroom," he said as he dumped the blankets on the floor. "Think you can make yourself comfortable with these?"

She shook her head. "I don't want to rest, thanks. There isn't any chance at all I'll sleep. If we've got to wait, let's talk."

"All right, but try lying down." He was straightening out the blankets on the floor. "Come on, do what you're told for once. I'll stick to the chair and keep watch, in case Jean comes round. She'll need some strong coffee and she'll probably be sick, but I don't think there'll be any other trouble with her—depending on what she remembers, which I hope won't be much."

"I told you, I shan't sleep," Helena said. But she lay down and all at once, as her muscles relaxed on the moderate comfort of the blankets, she felt the full extent of her weariness. Every part of her suddenly seemed to be aching.

But at least some of the ache was for Paul, as she knew when he knelt on the floor beside her, took her in his arms, kissed her forehead and then her mouth. Then quickly he drew away from her and went to the chair.

"Well, what shall we talk about?" he asked in the falsely casual voice which he seemed to imagine hid his feelings.

She was amused by that thought for a moment, amused that an emotional, vulnerable creature like Paul Forrest should imagine that he could ever hide anything. You only had to listen a little carefully to how he spoke, to watch the slight changes on his square, stubborn-looking face, to take some notice of how he used his hands, to know almost everything about him.

He was talking now, saying something about Denis and Marcia and what would happen when they came, and you knew that actually he was only doing it to put you to sleep, and again the transparency of it was amusing, but in a way that made you more inclined to cry than to laugh, it touched you so deeply. . . .

In less than five minutes Helena was sound asleep.

In fact it was three days before Denis and Marcia Forrest arrived in Tondolo. Igambo Airport had been closed to all traffic for that time. It had been impossible to telephone London and although cables had been accepted at the telegraph office, there had been no means of knowing if they were really being sent. The radio had talked incessantly of the success with which the army had put a stop to the civil war which had threatened the country as a result of the struggle for power between the traitor Kaggwa and the incompetent and corrupt Mukasa. Both these men, it was said, had been killed during the night of terror. Kaggwa in the fighting in the streets, Mukasa in his home, while resisting arrest, and a new era of honest government had now dawned in Uyowa under the strong and enlightened rule of General Ighodaro, who would protect freedom, put an end to corruption, and bring back true democratic rule at an early, though unspecified date. Meanwhile looting, not to mention seditious talk, would be severely punished.

Inexplicably, a wave of jubilation swept the city. There

were joyous demonstrations in the streets even before the corpses had been tidied away. Almost no one had heard of General Ighodaro before, but suddenly he was known to be the man who would put everything right. And you demonstrated, you shouted slogans, because after all you were alive.

A corpse that had not been tidied away when Paul drove Jean and Helena home in the early daylight after the fighting was one in a grey Vauxhall. The car had not got far. Helena recognised it, riddled with bullets, overturned by the side of the road. Inside it was a crumpled figure, lying twisted as no living person could lie. Paul did not pause and Helena quickly drew Jean's attention to a great pied crow, glossily black and white, on a bush on the other side of the road. Jean looked at the crow sleepily, nodded absently and yawned and leant her head against Helena's shoulder.

"It's very queer," she said, "the way I don't remember anything after seeing that waterfall. I remember the elephants, and the waterfall, and then it all just stops, until this morning."

"You had a touch of the sun," Paul said. "Don't worry about it."

"The sun? Have I had sunstroke? Really and truly sunstroke?"

"I think that's what we might call it," Paul said.

"Goodness! Sunstroke!" Jean seemed to feel a more important person for having this label to affix to her strange experience. "I remember Cleo, of course, and the drive. It was a lovely drive. I saw a marabou stork and some monkeys and some buffaloes—but I haven't seen a giraffe or a zebra or a lion yet. When am I going to see some giraffes and lions, Paul?"

"Any time you say, Jean," he answered. "We'll arrange it. I promise. Only don't go off on your own again, whatever you do. Will you promise that?"

"I wasn't alone, I was with Cleo," she said. "Where's she gone?"

"Away," he said.

"Why?"

"I suppose because she had to."

She sighed and closed her eyes. She was asleep again by the time that they reached home.

But she had taken in at least a little of the strangeness and desolation of the streets through which they had driven, for when she woke later, demanding Bongo and was told by her grandmother that Bongo was dead, she asked, "Did he die in battle?"

Mrs. Forrest said that he had and in spite of the great sadness that overcame Jean at the news, this seemed to give her a certain satisfaction, as there was satisfaction in the drama of having had sunstroke. Mrs. Forrest sat by her bed and would not let her out of her sight. Mr. Forrest roamed the garden, looked at the damage done by the digging there the night before, muttered at the sight of the strewn bricks of his pergola and made plans for the future.

"I'm not sure that I'll start that pergola again," he said, coming into the kitchen where Paul and Helena were cooking breakfast. "I didn't seem to have the hang of it. And the ground's been so thoroughly dug over, I think I might plant a few new shrubs there. A sisal, perhaps. We haven't got a really good one. . . . That bacon smells very good. So does that coffee. I wouldn't have thought it a few minutes ago, but I'm enormously hungry. I expect we'll all feel a lot better when we've had breakfast. . . ."

His mild voice talked them back to normality.

Later in the day Josiah came quietly back into the house and went about his work as abstractedly as usual, as deep as ever in his impenetrable dream. Towards evening Horace appeared. He was slightly drunk and even more inclined than usual to find the human scene a cause for continuous mirth, but he produced an excellent dinner of lamb chops with aubergines and tomatoes, followed by passionfruit ice cream. It was almost as if nothing had happened, except that Erasmus and Joe did not return. Once more, as she had on the day after the other battle, Helena felt herself being drugged into a misleading feeling that really nothing had happened. The last two days, she began to feel, had been a dream. Reality was this pleasant, airy house and quiet garden, the scent of tuberoses, jasmine and gardenias, the song of a bird, hidden among the purple and white posies of the potato tree, repeating over and over again in a soft, throaty coo, what sounded to her like the words "Come, come, I love you so."

Violence was only something that you heard about on the radio, and of which there would have been no need to hear if only Paul could have been persuaded to turn the thing off, instead of sitting glued to it for most of the day.

Several times during the day Mr. Forrest tried to telephone Robbie Meldrum, but the line remained dead. It was not until the late evening that the service was restored. They discovered it only when the bell started ringing, and it turned out that this was the superintendent himself, ringing up to ask how they had got through the night. He had heard of Jean's disappearance and also that the Forrests had been taken down to the police station and later released, but that was all. He would have been out to see them, he said, if he had had a moment.

"And now I'm just about dead on my feet. It's been one of the grimmest days I remember," he said. "Have you heard about the Passfields? Both of them killed, Peg with a spear in the house, Jim shot in the car when I suppose he was trying to get home, and all for no reason whatever. No looting done, even. But things seem to have quietened down for the present. It's a breathing space, if not much more. Shall I come up to see you?"

"I'd go home to Barbara, if I were you, Robbie," Mr. Forrest answered. "But we've a good deal we'd like to talk over with you when you've had some sleep. Some of it about the Passfields. Can you come to-morrow?"

"I'll do my best. Don't count on it, though. God knows what can still happen."

The night passed peacefully, however, and soon after breakfast Robbie Meldrum appeared and between them Paul and Helena told him of how they had found Jean in the Passfields' house and of what had happened there. When Paul mentioned that Jim Passfield had claimed to be up in the north getting the story of the same murders that

Meldrum himself had been investigating, he shook his head and said, "Never saw him. Can't have been there. Stupid sort of alibi, really. Too easy to blow sky high. But I don't suppose he expected to be here when I got back. Things didn't go too well for him, did they, what with a revolution and Miss Sebright's interference? If you hadn't stolen his car and arrived when you did, Miss Sebright, he might have got away with the child before the shooting really started." He turned to Paul. "What about your brother and his wife, Paul? How much do they know about all this?"

"If the cables we've sent off have got to them, nearly all of it," Paul answered, "but we haven't had any answers. I imagine they'll arrive as soon as planes are allowed to land again at Igambo."

"And you'll be leaving?"

"Soon," Paul said. "Not on the day I meant to, but pretty soon."

"Me too," Robbie Meldrum said. "When the army takes over, a sensible policeman gets out. I think Barbara and I could fancy a nice cottage in the Borders." He gave the long sigh of a deeply exhausted man. In spite of a night's sleep his ruddy face was sallow with fatigue. "You'll have to make an official statement about this Passfield business, of course, but at the moment I don't think anyone would be much interested in it."

He drove away.

"Talking of cottages," Paul said to his father, "mightn't this be a good time to track one down in Sussex?"

"Hm. Well. I suppose one might think about it," Mr. Forrest replied, with a quick look across the room towards the stairs. There was something furtive in the look, almost as if he were afraid that his wife, who was up there, reading to Jean, who was in bed, might hear him. "But you know the situation, Paul. Judy could never stand it. The climate, you know and—and everything."

Paul grinned and put a hand on his father's shoulder. "And everything," he said. He did not argue further.

It was Denis and Marcia, arriving on the first B.O.A.C. plane to land at Igambo, who tried to argue the elder

Forrests into leaving Uyowa. During the three days when no planes had been allowed to land, Denis had returned to London and so he and Marcia had arrived together. They had cabled the time of their arrival and Paul had gone to the airport to meet them.

He had not taken Jean, in spite of her protests. The streets were uneasy. Groups of soldiers patrolled them, sometimes good-humouredly, sometimes suddenly, and for no obvious reason, menacing. There was a lingering smell of smoke in the air and occasionally a fire, thought to have been put out, would flare up again.

One afternoon there were several loud explosions. Though this turned out to have been only some blasting on a new ring road that was being built round the town, the belief swept the city that the fighting was beginning again and the streets emptied themselves in a few minutes. Now and then a few shots would be heard, never explained, but renewing the sense of dread in the atmosphere.

The first time that Helena saw Marcia Forrest, a tall, bony woman in rumpled clothes, with untidy fair hair and a face of haggard and astonishing expressiveness rather than of beauty, she was in tears. She had just got out of the car that Paul had driven in at the gate and Jean had rushed to meet her. Jean started at once to tell her of all the marvels that she had seen and Marcia held her tight and let the tears pour down her face. Then Denis wanted to have Jean in his arms and Marcia turned to Mrs. Forrest, who had followed Jean out, and they embraced and both cried. No one would have dreamt that at least until that moment they had been sworn enemies.

Nor could they have guessed it during the next few days. Without discussion, some sort of agreement had been reached by the two women. It was based, of course, on Mrs. Forrest's surrender. During the two long days when she had stayed alone here in this house, she had fought some quiet battle of her own in the course of which she had succeeded at last in making herself yield her son and her grandchild to the stranger woman in the family. Even if she did not understand her or her way of life, even if her heart could never really warm to her, the war was over. It was peace, with a fair amount of honour on both sides, for Marcia, sens- ing her victory, did not flaunt it. She deferred to the older woman, was tactful, unexpectedly affectionate.

Helena thought that the truth about Marcia Forrest was that she was an unpractical, dependent and very affectionate woman, whose husband had had the perception, not to mention the strength of will, to keep her at her work because he had recognised that without it she would disintegrate. If they quarrelled, if their tempers sometimes raged and they threatened one another with divorce and convinced them- selves that they had grounds for it, it was only because two such people, both of them living on their highly strung nerves, would have to quarrel their way through life to keep any kind of balance. But they had only to meet some serious threat from the world outside their own private dramatic world of mock-strike to become one person.

However, Mrs. Forrest's whole nature had not changed overnight. If she had given up the hope of keeping her family round her, she had other plans for them which she expected should be carried out. Jean, she said, felt a certain sense of grievance that she had so far seen no giraffes, lions or zebras, and the place to see these was, of course, the National Game Park at Nairobi, which fortunately was not in a state of turmoil, like Tondolo, and so for the present was a far better place for a child. Denis, Marcia and Jean should depart to Nairobi as soon as possible; furthermore, they should take Helena with them, to make sure that she enjoyed at least some of her visit to Africa. Mrs. Forrest, it went without saying, would pay all the unexpected expenses that had arisen through the calamities of the last few days. And Paul? Paul of course would be going to London, where his arrival was already overdue.

The two brothers looked at one another over their mother's head, then Denis put his arms round her and kissed her.

"And you?" he said. "You and father? Why don't we all go back t-together?"

"Yes, why not?" Marcia said, sounding sincerely eager. "Then you could see lots more of Jean, and we could all

get to know one another properly. It would be wonderful.
Oh, do come!"

Both the elder Forrests nodded and smiled and said that
they would think about it. But later, separately, each explained in a lowered, confidential voice that the other could
never stand the change of climate, the change in everything to which they were accustomed. No doubt they would
return to England sometime, but not yet. Oh no, not yet.

"And if they ever do move," Paul said to Helena in the
morning of the day on which he was leaving, "if ultimately
they have no choice and are really driven out, they'll probably go to somewhere like Malta or Portugal, or even
Australia or New Zealand. They're frightened, you know,
they're really scared, of the new country Britain's turning into.
They won't feel nearly as out-of-date in the old, so-called
new countries. Incidentally, when you get back yourself. . . ."

"Well?" she said.

"If you'll let me know when you're arriving—but remember I'll be a very poor, overworked man by then—if I
can, I'll meet the plane."

He started to say something else, then stopped and she saw
a shadow on his face. It was the look that she had come to
think of as the Cleo look, and she knew that it might be a
long time before it finally faded. Meanwhile, he never
spoke of Cleo. Nobody spoke of her. When they mentioned,
which was rarely, the time when Jean had been missing, it
was as if they felt that the agony of it had been brought
about by some natural disaster, a hurricane or an earthquake,
not a human betrayal. Cleo was lost, gone, drowned deep,
left to the river.